Revenge and Wellness in the Sweet Hereafter

The Current Mr. Orr, Volume 3

Sean Boling

Published by Sean Boling, 2024.

REVENGE AND WELLNESS IN THE SWEET HEREAFTER

First edition. January 2, 2024.

Copyright © 2024 Sean Boling.

ISBN: 979-8223083016

Written by Sean Boling.

Chapter One

My letters to the living are handwritten. I deliver them by hand as well, and still manage to remain anonymous. I leave them when and where someone would not expect to find a letter from anybody, much less a letter from somebody who has spoken with a late loved one whose death left them with questions I try to answer.

Underneath the windshield wipers of parked cars is my top spot. I have also slid more than a few underneath doors. If I am feeling bold, and the parking lot or front yard is furnished with cameras, I pick a moment in public to make the drop and disappear before they read it. I leave the letter in their bag, or on their table while they are fetching a drink refill. When several minutes have passed, I walk back around to make sure they received it, and to watch their reaction upon reading the words.

Whether their eyes shed tears or grow large with shock, their next move is to look around to see who might have left it. I shield my identity with a variety of props. Glasses here, facial hair there, a hood pulled up, a cap pulled down, but not too far. I try not to look like someone trying to hide their face. Not many people recognize Devin Orr anymore. He has been out of the news for quite a while, but if he keeps showing up on security cameras or random phone videos whenever a letter is received, he would be back in the news, or at least the blogosphere.

There is an online community of those who have received a letter and those fascinated by them called *Receivers and Believers*. The founders of the site started by quoting and paraphrasing content from their letters, in particular the parts that make them look better than the dead.

For instance, the one about the deceased mother who became a conspiracy sponge in her later years and thought COVID was a hoax. Her daughter then brought her to places on purpose where she was likely to get the virus in order to prove a point. "I guess you won that argument," the mother jokes from the great beyond. On its own that would not prove paranormal contact, nor compel the daughter to share the letter I left on her windshield, since it implicates her for elder abuse. But the mother then proceeds to detail her many failings as a parent that inspired resentment in her daughter long before a virus paved the way to victory. In particular, my reference to her mother's "comparison compliments" convinced the daughter my letter was authentic, as in "That jacket is so cute; much cuter than that ugly one you wore to the reunion." Or "That's such a nice haircut; much nicer than that stupid one you had last Christmas." Those are also the parts, of course, that the daughter selected to post on the site.

The founders of the club in those early days also established how I sign the letters in the same manner: "From a fellow traveler with a unique passport." I still do. It offers a sense of brotherhood or sisterhood without referring to myself as a person or a friend, neither of which would be true.

Eventually members posted photos of their letters to compare the handwriting. They soon realized this was a terrible idea and took them down, but not before screenshots were circulated. Fraud kicked in. A batch of believers tried to pass themselves off as receivers. To help mitigate the damage, I became a member of the community under a stage name to plant doubts now and then about certain pretenders that my fellow subscribers seize on to unmask them. I can only do so much without drawing suspicion, so the number of receivers on the site remains inflated at roughly double the actual amount.

Other con artists were revealed when the community deduced over time that letters are delivered within a radius of about a hundred miles, with the valley as its epicenter. Early on when I started my commute between this world and the next, I asked Marlowe and his cohort to keep the contacts on earth as local as possible, given the logistics of locating and stalking them. Tracing my territory caused real estate to spike in a market that was already overheated, as people tried to buy their way into receiving a letter. When *Receivers and Believers* went from online curiosity to market force, a group of skeptics organized themselves into a competing community, *Deceivers of Believers*. The two rival clans bicker without having to worry over who is proven wrong or right, since they have to die to find out.

Only one Receiver has found out so far. A sweet older woman named Linea died not long after her husband traveled to the afterlife in a traffic accident that nearly killed them both. She spent her recovery distraught over how hard she pushed him to keep driving, long after it was safe, since she was uncomfortable with the idea of calling on unfamiliar cars with strangers behind the wheel. Linea and her husband were my first official case. Marlowe figured she would be joining him in the afterlife soon enough, and thought they would provide a helpful warmup before I took on more complicated fractures. All I had to do was pose as a caddy when he and his dead golf buddies would play one of the great courses of the world and birdie every hole. When I found myself alone with him, I would steer the conversation toward his wife, and by the eighteenth hole at his very own Pebble Beach, he acknowledged that driving while way too old was his fault as much as hers, maybe even more so, a final act of control over her that marked their marriage. He went on to share other examples, the worst being a long game of passive aggression he played to not only prevent Linea from finishing college when they met, but from going back to finish after their youngest daughter was an adult with a life of her own. He needed to feel superior, he confessed. He needed to feel in charge, always the one at the wheel, steering the ship, driving the car. I placed that revelation at the center of my letter to Linea, and it led to a happy enough reunion a year later when she made the leap due to natural causes.

They were my first case, but they were not my first letter. I wrote my first letter to Payton Lamp, the non-football playing son of Cam

Lamp, who was nonetheless featured prominently as the projection of a high school football player in his father's afterlife simulations. In a twist of fate well worth the wait, Payton ended up being the founding member of *Deceivers of Believers*. He used my letter, which he claims to have dismissed out of hand, as the cornerstone of his mission.

The Payton Lamp letter was also the only one inspired by a visit demanded by Trisha rather than suggested by Marlowe. My orders from Trisha were to visit his father to raise dirt on her mother, but I ended up with a lot of sympathy for the Lamps, and not just because Trisha's mother killed the elder Lamp with a heaping mouthful of flourless chocolate torte. When Payton's website first came to my attention, his disbelief in my letter was not what worried me. *Receivers and Believers* needed a foil. The doubt sowed by *Deceivers of Believers* provides me with additional camouflage, and while letter fraud lingers and housing prices hover well above a rational number, both would be even worse without the *Deceivers* keeping a cold finger on the pulse of the *Receivers*. No, my initial worry was the connection between Payton and Trisha.

Through some oblique questioning of Trisha, I learned that my worries were unfounded. Stepbrother and stepsister never even met while Cam was still alive and married to Trisha's mother, whose name Trisha never uses. Their parents wed in a Reno courthouse with a Justice of the Peace presiding. The only way Trisha would catch Payton's eye is if he instead believed my letter and somehow linked it to her cloning lab, while the only way Payton would catch Trisha's eye is if he owned shares in a competing business in the valley and had once slighted her. Neither of those angles are coming to pass, so I can rest assured they will stay in their corners. He keeps using his status as the original Receiver to foam at the mouth over the authenticity of the letters I leave, while she continues to keep me in a psychic harness, ready to sic me on yet another competitor she has convinced herself is an enemy.

Every time I check in for my next unleashing, she has added a new feature to her office complex. Sculptures, aquariums, and art installations play the role of scalps nailed to a wall.

The latest is a terrarium in the lobby that takes up more space than most offices.

I peer through the glass at the woodsy wetlands, a gathering of ferns and redwood husks lining a series of shallow waterways joined by a gentle current. It takes me a minute to notice the little brown lizards lounging in the shallows and on the mossy rocks that break the surface.

I never see any of the people whose lives I ruin on her behalf, much less write them letters. I bring back information, Trisha concocts a strategy to profit from it, then someone else carries out the plan. Sometimes I feel as though I am flying back from the afterlife in a B-52, dropping my bombs from high above the clouds, watching them disappear into the fluff before I go home and hear about the damage much later.

"They're clones," Trisha says from behind me.

"What?" I keep my eyes on the humid habitat inside the glass walls. "The lizards?"

"Newts," she corrects me. "Part of the salamander family. They live on both land and water. Can't make up their minds."

"Why clone a newt?"

"One of my fellow board members has land up north in the redwoods that he wants to build a house on, but some endangered newts were there first. He needs to make sure they're not endangered on his property."

"Are your clones going to breed with the native population or destroy them?" I watch one of the newts climb out of the water.

"We shall see."

"That's not like you to help someone," I turn to face her. "Even if your help may ruin an ecosystem."

"He came to me. I'm a person of note."

"Which board?"

"One with a lot of retirees. Former people of note."

"You're running out of prey."

"That's why you're going to visit Tip Galvan this time. Let's go."

She turns and heads for the elevator.

As I follow her across the lobby, I focus on the train of crepe that flows behind her and wonder what would happen if I stepped on it. More than likely it would rip, but maybe it would hold, and after a few steps she would suddenly jerk backwards, like a dog maxing out a chain that is staked into the ground. Or maybe she would spin like a top, a whirling dervish of chiffon unraveling from around her, layer after layer, a dance of seven veils, or however many layers she may wear.

"Have you ever met Tip?" she asks as I catch up and we board the elevator.

"Devin has, according to a couple of his memories."

"Separate encounters? Or from the same meeting?"

"I don't know," I say as the doors slide shut. "But I never met him. He was out of the game by the time I started the charity and might have hit him up."

"I'm sure you'll ingratiate yourself to him better than Devin ever could. You and Tip are a lot alike. He was the kind of venture capitalist who didn't need to know exactly how the technology worked, just what it could do for people. And he knew exactly how people worked."

The doors open and she leads the way as usual.

"That doesn't mean he knew how to extract secrets from them," I chase her.

"He didn't have to," she struts ahead down the hall. "His research team dug up everything there is to know about the people he was thinking of investing in, as well as the people who had already put in money, or were considering it. His nearly spotless investment track record speaks to the scope of that research."

"Did he invest in you?"

"In my company, you mean?"

"So that's a no."

"I never approached him."

"Really?" I poke. "Because I'll ask him."

"You know my policy. Do whatever you want over there, so long as you come back here with what I asked for."

I scoff with purpose.

She stops and faces me.

"Sure," I answer her face. "Whatever I want. How many days early are you going to pull me out this time?"

She sizes up the lies she has lined up for this occasion.

"I have concerns about your long-term health," she chooses to say.

"You're trying to find the sweet spot."

She cocks her head to one side to clear the way for further explanation.

I oblige.

"The right amount of time for me to get what you want, but not enough for me to get what I want."

Her response is to start walking again.

I consider heading in the opposite direction before following again.

"Speaking of what you want," she says as we turn a corner. "An interesting story popped up in my news feed. A crunchy, touchy-feely puff piece about people receiving letters from their dead enemies."

"Dead loved ones," I correct her. "Loved ones they had unresolved issues with."

"Like there's any other kind," she snorts. "Does it help?"

"In some cases, I think."

"It sure didn't help my dear stepbrother. Ex-stepbrother, I guess. People stop being step-siblings after a parent dies, I assume. You didn't tell him about my mother, did you?"

"Don't you think they would have mentioned a murder in the article?"

"I decide when and if she goes to jail," she reminds me.

"I'm surprised it took you this long to discover the great letter caper."

"The algorithm knows I never click on gauzy human interest stories. Not sure how this one broke through."

"The name Lamp, perhaps?"

"We should all hang out sometime," she muses. "You, me, and Cammy Junior. What's his name again?"

I suspect she knows, but I remind her anyway.

"Payton."

We reach her office and she sifts through her crepe for the key.

"I've had so many wins in a row," she ignores his name. "So many easy wins, I need some tension in my life."

Someone slides their arms under mine and presses their hands onto the back of my head.

"Donnie?" I ask.

"In the flesh," he verifies. "Unlike you, freak."

"Donnie, please," Trisha sounds like she may be rolling her eyes, but I cannot tell since my head is being forced to look downward.

"I'm not going to resist, Donnie."

"I'm re-creating the element of surprise."

"Well, ya got me."

I collapse into a freefall and we both drop to the floor.

"Doesn't this provide you with enough tension?" I ask Trisha after we land. "Thinking up ways to put me under?"

"Donnie and I collaborate on that."

"I didn't know you were capable of collaboration."

"Careful, clone," Donnie hisses. "I've got a needle pressed to your neck."

And so he does.

"I don't remember you being this angry, Donnie. Is there a problem at work?"

"I love my job," he jabs me with the needle.

"I get it," I feel the numbness spread. "The boss is here. We'll talk when I get back."

"Write him a letter," Trisha quips as the lab coats arrive during my fade to black.

Even if I could speak, I have no comeback.

Chapter Two

"Maybe she's right," I lament to Marlowe as I stab my straw into a glass of iced tea.

"I shiver at the thought of agreeing with Trisha about anything," Marlowe says. "But you know how I feel about the letters."

"I'm not sure how I feel about your new look."

Marlowe is posing as a femme fatale this time, as opposed to the hard-boiled detective façade he likes to wear. Along with a red dress, brunette bangs, and horn-rimmed sunglasses, she speaks in a breathy voice.

"That's the point," she lowers her sunglasses and looks over the top of them at me. "Catch you off guard, scramble your defenses, but at the same time look professional."

"A professional what?"

"Secretary."

"Nobody calls them that anymore."

"They do here."

"On the planet they're called assistants. And they don't dress like that."

"They do in the simulations our residents build."

"And I suppose they also call them 'honey' and 'baby' and 'doll'?"

"More often than not," she concedes.

"We need to find a way to send you to earth for a while. Learn how it currently works."

She sighs and switches back to the trench coat, fedora, and male persona.

"How did I do with the restaurant this time?" he asks.

"Very nice."

I almost mean it. He has combined concepts, as he often does, that would never attract investors on earth, but makes for a vivid thought experiment. This time he has gone with haute French cuisine in a sports bar setting. The screens hung high on the walls that encircle the dining room play every sport from different seasons at once, while elderly waiters in bow ties deliver dishes covered in metal domes.

"Why do you feel the need to catch me off guard and scramble my defenses?" I ask.

"It just so happens I was planning on encouraging you to talk to our targets, rather than slip them notes."

"Targets," I zero in on the word. "We should really come up with a new name for them."

"Patients?"

"We're not doctors."

"You're stalling," he accuses. "Avoiding the subject."

"Subjects," I pounce. "That's a promising word."

"When you were bellyaching over Trisha teasing you about the letters, I thought it was fate, that we were meant to finally hash this out."

"That you didn't need the doll-face, honey-baby façade after all."

"That's how desperate we've become."

"We?"

"The board isn't big on the letters, either."

"The letters work."

"One of them worked. For one case."

"The first case. A sign of good things to come."

"The smallest possible sample size."

"Don't reduce Linea like that."

"We're not the ones using her as anecdotal evidence."

"I know," I lean back and give up drinking. "And I get it. I'd love to never write another letter, but I don't know how else to approach the targets, the patients, the subjects. How do you verbalize the kind of message I come bearing without sounding like a lunatic? Or a cult leader?"

"Nobody ever suggested you should tell them where you've been. We don't want them to know that. Plus, you're right. It would sound insane."

"I could pretend to be one of those people who says they can communicate with the spirit world. That would put me in fine, upstanding company. I could hold court in a yurt out in the desert, or in a crumbling condemned apartment building where people have to walk through several doorways hung with beaded curtains to reach me."

"We're not asking for anything of the sort."

"Then what?"

"Why not befriend the people left behind? Get to know them? Like you did with Jane's husband and her kids, and with Phil's parents."

"Devin knew Jane and knew Phil. Their families were bound by the same foundation started in Phil's name. Devin can't start showing up on the doorsteps of random people with offers of legacy charities named after the dead they're mourning, or cursing."

"Maybe he could if you hadn't started with the letters," he mutters a side swipe.

"It wouldn't be any less suspicious under any circumstances," I let him know I can hear him.

"You're built to charm," he overcorrects into sweet talk. "You've said so yourself. Take the information you learn about them in the afterlife and use it in small doses, when it's most effective. Present it as a hypothetical, or speculation. Like, 'I'll bet your Nana loved it when you complimented her kahlua ham.' That sort of thing."

"So weeks, months of massaging them to deliver a message that isn't even direct. We can't compete with Trisha at that rate."

"We've given up competing with Trisha. It's time to focus on quality rather than quantity. That's why lately we've been running with only-children only."

"Only-children only…"

The term strikes me as a mouthful.

"No siblings," he clarifies.

"Ah," I grasp the definition and the strategy. "So we have. Tighter circle. Less chance for detection."

"Correct," he signs off on my assumption. "We decided that was the move when we found ourselves considering a woman who left behind twelve children."

"The extreme can make the obvious more clear."

"Eleven of them hate her," he adds. "All except the youngest."

"Why not the youngest?"

"She kept having children because she liked being a mother to babies and little kids, but didn't care much for the part where they got older. When she died, the youngest was still in her sweet spot."

"That's a lot of letters," I spend a second wondering if I could have pulled it off.

"And a non-starter for any face-to-face meetings. Reaching out to any one kid carried an exponential amount of risk. It was a reminder we were all a bit too excited at first. Over our skis. Is that the right expression?"

"One of many that apply," I lament.

"We appreciate that you were as hopeful as we were."

Our waiter appears and hunches over to take our order.

"We're only having drinks today," Marlowe tells him.

"No food?" the old fellow raises his ample eyebrows.

"No," Marlowe confirms. "But we'd like a refill."

The server sighs and shuffles off.

"I don't think we're getting a refill," I narrate his exit.

"I gathered that crabbiness is part of the experience in a place like this," Marlowe explains.

"Your innocence is charming," I toss the straw from my glass to drain what's left of my iced tea. "And I don't mean when it comes to designing restaurants. I mean when it comes to wanting to help people."

I take the bottom sip and discover there was more tea in the glass than I thought and the gulp punches my throat on its way down.

"My innocence is willfully ignorant," I push through the discomfort. "I knew what was coming. Blackmailing people is a lot easier than healing them. If I had any hope that it was the other way around, or roughly the same, Trisha squished it right away. She doesn't talk to her targets, either. She has people who work for her send messages and handle the transactions."

"Damning information plays well when it comes from a mysterious source."

"While uplifting information should be more personal. I see your point."

Rather than revel in his victory, Marlowe offers assurances.

"Your letters have made a mark," he says.

"They've sparked a debate," I counter.

"The people you contacted will be very happy when they finally get their answer. Like Linea."

"In the meantime they'll be stuck in a war of words between their enablers and the doubters, living life in perpetual antagonism, us versus them. Think pieces I read often use the great Receivers vs. Deceivers stalemate as an example of everything wrong with rhetoric in the online era."

Marlowe has no reply, having emptied his pockets of platitudes.

"You know what would really set us up?" I seize the silence.

"No," he already knows what I am going to propose.

"We'd breeze past Trisha if you'd allow it."

"The ghost portal is to communicate with you, and you only."

"What if Trisha decides she doesn't need me anymore?"

"Then you'll be able to tell us through the ghost portal on the first Monday of the month at two in the afternoon."

"And I can bring someone with me to talk directly to their friend or loved one."

"Then every mystical pixie in the world is drawn to it like a beacon and they turn that vending machine into sacred ground."

"It's closer to the ice machine."

"We can't have people thinking the afterlife is a country they can immigrate to. No."

"Anyone who uses the portal has to take a vow," I suggest.

"Now your innocence is surpassing mine."

"They sign a contract."

"And what happens if they break it? You may hang out with the dead, but you're not a killer. Why are you so determined not to spend time with our subjects?"

"Truth is," I pave the way for my confession. "It's a lot of work. I have all my earth errands to do on top of what we do. I have to play Devin and run my charity."

"One person at a time. That's all we're asking at this point."

He gives me room to ponder. I take him up on it for a moment and feel ashamed, so I exit the space he provides and instead watch a football game playing on the screen most aligned with my field of vision.

"Is this a recording of a game that was actually played?" I ask.

"It's a simulation," he shakes his head. "Based on the millions of possibilities every move creates."

"There's a score. One team is ahead. Are those points randomly assigned?"

"No. A model plays out and its current status is revealed when you look at the screen."

"So there are no games on the screens behind me right now?"

"Not until you pay attention to them."

"I suppose if I had a favorite team, it would win all the time."

"Not necessarily."

"Most of the time, on their way to a championship."

"The big fans do that, especially when their team never won anything in their lifetime, but it gets old, and some even find the struggle was more satisfying than the ring, so they go back to letting their team lose."

"Naturally," I may as well slap myself in the forehead. "I've been around the afterworld enough to know."

I look at a different screen that plays a baseball game. The pitcher winds up and throws a fastball that nearly beans the batter. The batter barks at the pitcher and steps toward the mound.

"I know people can't harm each other here," I am reminded. "Not physically. I tried with Devin once."

We share some soft laughter.

"But how far do people push the limits?" I brush past my laugh. "Have they tried to kill each other? Real people, residents sharing a simulation."

"Sometimes it's the first thing they try to do," he agonizes. "They accept an invitation, or extend one, and make their move. It's one of the more stark reasons we wanted to work with you."

"And I take it they can't draw their gun when they try, or swing their bat, or whatever they want to use."

"Sometimes they can follow through if it's not detected at the very moment. There's almost always an emotional buildup, so usually by the time it happens they get that invisible restraint like I imagine you did."

"I did."

"But sometimes a resident simply snaps. Or if it's premeditated, and they're a psychopath, they remain calm. When that happens, it may take a second to get a signal. If so, the bullet then passes through the intended victim, or the blow from the blunt object feels like a light slap when it lands. Why do you ask? Are you thinking of taking another shot at Devin?"

"No," I fall into a little more laughter. "It's just that I'm never here for very long, and I spend my time with people who can stay as long as they want. I watch how they conduct themselves, and regardless of whether I think they're doing a good job or not, I wonder how meaningful a life can be that ends strictly by choice."

"Most of our residents get off to a shaky start, lots of depravity and decadence, but eventually a lot of them also build simulations filled with purpose."

"I used the word 'meaning'."

"On purpose?"

"Yes," I allow his joke. "On purpose. I think there is a difference, and having both is best."

"Why don't you think our residents can have them both?"

"I can't speak for them, and I don't get to know them well enough to ask them. But part of the reason I was so enamored with this place on my first visit is because I didn't know if I'd be allowed to stay. Then later on, when I learned I was going to be pulled back to earth, I didn't know when that would be. I see people develop purpose here, like you said, maybe even meaning. Maybe I'm wrong and the words are interchangeable. Let me try 'value' instead. I can't help thinking that without the possibility of life ending at any moment, its value is reduced."

"Good thing you're wondering and not asking," Marlowe says. "My existence never ends, so what do I know?"

"Existence," I take note of his word choice. "That's an interesting way to put it."

"Is it a life if it never ends?"

I have even less to offer him on the perils of immortality than he may have to offer me on the nature of meaning, or purpose, or value.

We sit in silence at our impasse.

I swerve around it by getting down to business.

"So what do you have for me?" I ask.

"Just one this time," he is grateful to talk shop.

"In the interest of cultivating a relationship," I assume.

"A son whose mother outlived him."

"He must not be a kid if he made it here."

"He's an adult, yes. And most of his adult life was spent putting his mom through a lot of stress. He's concerned about how she's coping back on the planet. From what we've been able to assemble, she lives a life that gives you plenty of opportunities to get close to her and help her deal with with his disappearance."

"She doesn't know he's dead?"

"She probably does by now. I'll let Elijah give you the details."

"That's his name?"

"He prefers Eli."

"No concern for his father?"

"To put it mildly. The father arrived here recently, but Eli wants nothing to do with him. Didn't even request an appointment when the old man arrived."

"Then I take it there's also tension between the widow and late husband."

"There is, but none of the affected parties are interested in resolving it."

"Huh," I punctuate my wonder.

"Don't."

"What?"

"The father, the husband, he played neither of those roles well."

"With no regrets?"

"If his simulations are any indication."

"Huh," I deepen my wonder.

"Don't."

"What?"

"Please leave him out of it. Focus on the mother and the son. June and Eli."

"What if I have some free time? Learning about the situation as a whole might help with the particulars."

"Fine," he sighs. "His name is Pep Rivers."

"So the mother's name is June Rivers?"

"Yes."

"The marriage may not have been ideal, but she got a great name out of it."

"Pep spends most of his time in the simulation of a luxury wellness spa he tried to develop out in the desert, or pretended to develop. He relied so heavily on cons and schemes it's difficult to say if he ever really intended to build it."

"Pep," I spend time with his name.

"Yep."

"Perfect. I also have just one resident Trisha wants to tap, and his name's Tip. Tip and Pep."

"Pep is not the goal," he reminds me.

"Can't I enjoy those two names next to each other for a moment?"

"Tell me about this Tip she wants to tap."

"Tip Galvan. Legendary venture capitalist. Trisha is running out of targets, and she thinks he can provide her with a whole new list."

"How so?"

"He invested in a boatload of successful startups, thanks in large part to his crack research team. Trisha is banking on there being more to that research than benchmarks and burn rates. I hope she's right. If Tip does have a fat list of rascals, I'll use it to combat the time squeeze she keeps tightening around my visits. I can memorize as many of the marks as possible, then bring her one at a time and focus on your missions when I'm here."

The possibility energizes Marlowe.

"Tip should be easy to find," he claims.

He lapses into a blank stare for a moment.

"In fact," his eyes regain their spark. "We just did. Ready for Tip?"

The waiter appears.

"Wrong Tip," Marlowe lets him down. "We're still working here, thank you."

The waiter mutters off.

Marlowe looks embarrassed.

"I would never plant a joke that corny in a simulation," he swears. "You know that."

"I know you had a jukebox play 'Only You' when you first met me," I tease.

"That was spontaneous. I said I would never plant a joke like that, as in program it, on purpose."

"Maybe he really did overhear us," I reach for Occam's razor to cut through his defenses.

"He can barely hear us when he's standing next to the table."

"We did say Tip's name several times."

"Probably one of my colleagues. Their idea of a joke. Or it could be a glitch. If I can't get anyone to confess, I'll talk to Maintenance and Operations."

"How about Eli?" I navigate us back to business. "What does he like to simulate? So I know where to go after I visit Tip."

I brace myself with a wince and look around for the waiter, but whoever or whatever pulls his strings has let the joke run its course.

"Eli spends a lot of time in a bar playing in a band."

"Not a sold out arena?"

"Humility is the overriding theme of his simulations."

"Very few places to sit?" I develop a picture of the bar. "Somehow more dark corners than actual corners? Every square foot of the walls covered in gifts from beverage company sales reps and photos of customers?"

"That should get you there."

"If it were earth, I'd include the smell of nicotine and mopped up beer."

"He may have kept that."

"You don't have a sense of smell?"

"I haven't dropped in on him. One of my colleagues brought him to our attention."

"Do you know anything about his band?"

"They're a Slipknot tribute band called Burlap."

"Slipknot," I consider the implications.

"You're familiar with them?" Marlowe clearly is not.

"I'm familiar with their merchandise."

"Based on the name, I assume it's either Country and Western wear, or gory and suggestive hoodies."

"The latter."

"I can only imagine what the music sounds like."

"You'll find out eventually. Their fans aren't getting any younger. Any idea where I'm dropping in on Tip?"

"A very different kind of bar."

"How so?"

"Bring small bills for the tip jar."

Before he finishes his sentence, I see a tip jar on the table, but rather than a jar, it is an extra-large brandy snifter.

At the end of his sentence, Marlowe is gone, and the brandy snifter is no longer on our table, but on top of a grand piano.

The bills, for the most part, are not small. There are ones and fives, but they are outnumbered by tens and twenties.

I am sitting on a barstool alongside the piano. I still have a glass in front of me, but it is shorter and filled with what looks like iced tea but is more likely a spirit, either whiskey or bourbon.

The woman at the piano sings "Autumn Leaves". She keeps her playing simple, relying on long pauses between chords to emphasize her voice. I listen for a few bars to help me settle into the simulation before I scan the room for Tip.

He is seated across the piano from me, eyes closed, soaking in the atmosphere, alone. I assumed I would have to imagine a younger version in order to identify him, but he looks as old as he was when he died at the end of his lengthy, successful life. Interrupting his reverie would be rude and probably unproductive, so I wait until he appears more present, which only happens after another song, when the piano player takes a break and excuses herself with a promise to return.

I am tempted to slip into the piano player projection and experience playing the piano and singing, but I let her go and stick with my policy when it comes to Trisha missions.

I never disguise myself when working for her. I conduct her business with utmost transparency, going so far as to announce what I am, and who I am working for, in the hope that when she arrives in the afterlife, she has a miserable experience, greeted by a horde of resentful residents anxious for a word with her.

Tip recognizes me before I make my move.

His recognition moves from surprise to irritation.

I nod at him, and when he nods back, I walk around to his side of the piano.

"You were too young," he offers his condolences before addressing my impropriety. "But I didn't invite you, and you never sent me a request."

"I'm his clone," I reach out to shake his hand. "But you can still call me Devin."

"Devin Orr had a clone," he studies my hand during our brief shake.

"To do all the things he didn't want to do."

"Like spending time with people?"

"Mainly during crunch."

"So we have met before."

"That was him. I came after that meeting. I think. He would have seized any chance to meet with you even if I was available. Which I can relate to."

"To what do I owe this pandering?"

"I'm here thanks to an accidental discovery made through the lab owned by Trisha Miter. I can move between life on earth and the life to come."

"Let me guess," he sincerely wants to make a prediction. "They put you under some sort of cryogenic suspension and it simulates death."

"That about sums it up."

"Remarkable," he seems to want to touch my face.

"And here I was told you're more of a people person than a tech guy," I lean back a bit to signal I would prefer he keep his hands to himself.

"I couldn't help but learn a thing or two over the years," he catches himself staring. "But this...you."

"A bit of a leap."

"Last I checked cloning was still just sheep."

"Did you ever invest in it?"

"I was rarely approached. They tend to apply for state and federal grants. Their return on investment takes too long."

"Not for Trisha. She blew up the timeline."

"By accident," he echoes my earlier revelation.

I concur with a nod before further clarifying.

"By sending me here for information she can use to blackmail people."

He leans back and howls with laughter loud enough to draw stares from the projections that surround us at the main bar and dining room.

"Perfect," he narrates his reaction.

"So you know Trisha."

"Never met her," he settles into slumping over his drink. "But I know this place."

"That doesn't sound like a flattering assessment."

He takes a sip and sits up straight, stretching and gathering his thoughts.

"Maybe it's because I started doing business in the valley back when it was merely a place where a lot of technology companies were located, and not a so-called cradle of innovation, but I don't fit the stereotype. Not the current one."

"How so?" I ask. "Or how not so?"

"I was a devout Christian. I think I still am. But I have yet to find a single clue that any of my beliefs were true."

"Well," I calibrate how I might comfort him. "Just because Jesus hasn't been able to hang out in your simulation doesn't mean he's not here. He must get millions of invitations."

"We shouldn't have to invite him."

"I'm sure it's the same with Muhammed and Buddha, and Joseph Smith."

"My poor wife," he laments. "My darling Missy. She'll be far more devastated than I am when she gets here. She's the one who introduced me to Christ."

"I have a friend named Phil," I think of something that might help. "I met him on my first visit to the afterlife, and he has an interesting theory on how this place works."

"Oh really?"

"He's convinced that this is the real test. Earth was the semester, and this is the final exam, with a single prompt: How do you behave when it appears to have been proven that no one is watching, or no one cares, and you can do whatever you want?"

"A theory," Tip mulls the term. "So he's put this idea through rigorous experimentation."

"No."

"So it's a hypothesis."

"I stand corrected."

"And I'm supposed to deny Jesus for a guy named Phil."

I laugh.

He does not.

"I didn't mean it like that," I refer to my laugh and Phil's hypothesis all in one. "Forgive me. I haven't been around for very long. A couple of years total on earth, give or take a month, and who knows how long here, where time doesn't exist. I'm good at persuading people to believe me, but I have a hard time understanding belief in someone else, or something else."

He appears to assess my apology.

"As long as you deliver for Trisha," he proves to be assessing my situation instead. "You can keep traveling back and forth. Am I right?"

"As usual."

His assessment continues for an extended silence.

"If there is no God," he concludes. "We'll have to fill that void. Let's smite some sinners."

"Are you sure?"

"You have that much faith in Phil?"

"I don't want you to abandon your faith on my account."

"Let's put it this way, then. If I was the Christian I thought I was, there are people I never should have invested in. I gave a lot of my money to the church and to charity, but the way I earned it still matters."

He chugs the rest of his drink in one throbbing sip.

"Are you going to take notes?" he gulps for air. "Or do you memorize?"

"I take notes," I produce a pen and pad of paper. "Then I memorize them."

The piano player takes her seat and strikes a chord to announce her presence.

"Let's go someplace quiet," Tip suggests.

He drops a twenty in the snifter and I follow him through the dining room and out the French doors to a brick patio in a forest overlooking a lake.

"People love being next to the water," I remark.

"Home sweet home," he scans the surface. "We should have never dragged ourselves onto land."

"Your crisis of faith is taking fire on all fronts."

"I never bought into the creation side of it."

We both give the large body a long look.

"You want all the scumbags at once?" he asks at last. "Or should we give her a slow drip?"

I explain my preference for the slow drip, hoarding a backlog of backstabbers so that I may pay more attention to the good work I try to do while in the afterlife.

"Good work?" he wants details.

"Getting to know residents who left people in pain on earth and finding ways to resolve it."

"Isn't everyone left with some pain when someone close to them dies?"

"I'm not talking about the pain of loss."

"Of unsettled disputes," he catches on.

"That's right."

"And this is a regular part of these business trips you take?"

"It is."

"How's that part going?"

"The good work is a lot harder than the bad work."

Our conversation reaches a light switch inside of him.

He clicks it on.

"You must need permission from those in charge to jump around between all these simulations."

"I have it."

He looks hopeful.

"There are a lot of levels," I break it to him. "And I work with one close to the bottom."

He looks let down.

"I wish I could introduce you to someone who can prove your faith," I try to make him feel better. "But those I work with really are interested in making things right for people back home, and all of your intelligence would help a great deal."

"A diversion," he broods.

"Which beats pining around here aimlessly."

Tip scans the horizon for something to keep him from seeing my point.

"If your friend Phil is correct," he eases his way back into our scheme. "This is a good way to hedge my bets."

In the interest of dispensing both justice and healing, he recites a list of a dozen dirty candidates for me to choose from, along with a verbal thumbnail of each to summarize why they qualify. I jot them all down, but for the first drop in our slow drip to Trisha, I narrow my choices down to three.

In the process, we realize that while we have options that reside upstream, close to the sources of wealth and power, I have eliminated them in favor of targets who sift through the shallows farther downstream. Our strongest possibilities need to be involved in scandals that are relatable and easy to understand, so if they are revealed, public sentiment turns quickly. The transactions of those higher up the stream tend to be convoluted and require knowledge of subjects people find boring, things like water rights, land use legislation, banking regulations, tax laws, tariffs, homestead acts, county supervisor purviews. Their scandals take a long time to explain, are prone to being tuned out even by those making an honest effort to learn about them, and fail to inspire slogans and trashy storylines. They are written in legalese, not prose, much less poetry. Our most promising candidates have wronged persons, not taxpayers. They hold positions that the public can imagine themselves in, and imagine making the moral choice, rather than the ones our contenders made.

Now with less to memorize, Tip provides me with more detail on those left standing.

We have the administrator of a psychiatric hospital who also sits on the board of directors for a medical device company. He granted conservatorship over a patient to the chairman of that lucrative board. The patient is the chairman's niece, who checked herself in and was not chronically disturbed, just having a bad day, which she often did since her father died and left her with an enormous inheritance. Her uncle, the chairman, offered to manage it for her, but she thought it wise to separate family and funds. She was right. Her captivity proves it.

We have the art dealer who manipulates the provenance of stolen antiquities and sells them to the newly-wealthy scattered about the valley. His most profitable pipeline runs between those who perceive themselves as self-made with sculptures depicting hyper-masculine demigods dishing out vengeance on any and all who have slighted them in the slightest. The victims of their violence are never seen. Depictions of their shrieking death fail to make the cut into the stone or metal. Only the victor remains.

We have the beneficiary of family wealth amassed from real estate holdings owned for generations in a tourist-trap beach town. Cash has flowed from the chintzy souvenir shops and musty restaurants into his family trust for almost a century, but he extracts a bonus revenue stream from those same moldy sources by threatening the owners of those reliable relics with newer, trendier, higher-end development unless the old friends of his family contribute monthly to his "Seaside Heritage Preservation Fund", a non-licensed nonprofit that claims to lobby on behalf of longtime lease holders.

"All three are going down eventually," I ponder the nominees from our lake view perch. "But do you think they should be delivered in any particular order?"

"Can't go wrong in any direction," he maintains. "They all ensnare multiple people beyond the lead player."

"That could be my criteria. Rank them from widest net to tightest net."

"The art dealer is the widest. You not only get all his buyers, you get his family. They're from Moldova and none of them want to go back."

"As for the order, I think tightest to widest would be best. If I lead with the bigger catches, Trisha might see the next rounds as diminishing returns."

"Then start with the psych hospital administrator and his crony chairman of the board. That's the tightest. The king of the tourist trap also leads to his family, and other families for that matter. There's a whole cabal of tasteless old tightwads in that eyesore of a town. Plus with the hospital administrator, you get to rescue the niece who's stuck in that godforsaken ward."

"Trisha won't care about that. She'll let them pay her extra to keep that poor woman in there."

"You could make it a condition."

"I have nothing to do with how she uses the information."

"You could try."

"Did you?" I snip.

"Fair point," Tip exhales in the direction of the lake. "I may not have used the info to leverage anyone, but I ignored it."

"How did you even unearth all this dirt?"

"Various startups I was considering had someone on their team connected to this den of thieves. Sometimes it was tangential, like the engineering design consultant for one company who bought a bust from the Moldovan. Others were direct participants, potential fellow investors, like the gift shop mafia don who was looking for a return on his shakedown money, or the star of our first act, the psychiatric hospital administrator who ended up as one of the largest shareholders in the medical device company thanks to his well-informed, professional opinion regarding the chairman's niece."

"I'll see what I can do," I make him a probably-empty promise.

"You'll feel better," he insists.

"Even if ending the conservatorship is a non-starter," I remind him. "I still have some good work to pursue."

He simulates a smile and looks out at the lake.

"First me," he sticks with the lake. "Then the good stuff."

"Trisha's contacts are always the first stop. I need to make sure I can come back."

"It's not the order that bothers me."

I survey the view for something more soothing to say than what I have said so far.

"Would you like me to check in on your wife?" I ask. "Deliver a message to Missy?"

"No need," he calls off my search. "I'll hold out. She's worth the wait."

Tip makes his way back to the piano bar.

"Good luck with the good stuff," he says as he opens the door.

I hear the singer crooning "Between the Devil and the Deep Blue Sea" for a moment before he shuts it behind him.

Chapter Three

I imagine the bar where Eli plays as an exception to the rule of water, a simulation nowhere near any lakes, rivers, or seas.

Walls rise in front of Tip's lake, a roof slides over the walls, and projections appear. The brick floor of the patio is the last feature to fade, giving way to flat cement coated in a sticky veneer of fossilized spilled drinks.

It adheres to many of the assumptions I made. There are precious few places to sit, very low lighting, and very little square footage remaining on the walls among the liquor promos, photos of bands that played there frequently, and of customers who drank to excess.

Its quality as a music venue is the biggest surprise. The stage is roomy and appears to have its own system of amplifiers stacked on each side, with a lengthy scaffold of lights running across the top. The quality of the music is hard to say. I am not the target audience. The projections in attendance nod their heads and raise their fists. They were made to like it. Lyrics are screamed over a bass line heavy enough to either cause or cure a cardiac arrest, while the drums roll like a wheel of fortune that keeps spinning at high speed.

Each member of the band wears a different costume, their faces hidden by masks. The bass player is a bear wearing a necktie. One guitarist is a clown dressed in a prison onesie, the other wears a horse head and a police uniform. The DJ and synth player are decked out in matching little girl party dresses and identical oversized human heads with no hair and bulging eyes. The drummer wears the titular burlap sack over his head. The exception is the lead singer, who is dressed in a standard bar band ensemble of jeans , t-shirt with the logo of another band on it, and no mask.

"Is the lead singer named Eli?" I shout at the nearest projection mechanically bopping his head.

He appears to give one of his bops an extra nod.

"Is that a yes?" I shout.

He augments his nodding with a raised thumb.

"Thanks," I stop shouting.

I walk the floor to see if there is a projection I would like to inhabit. One song into my study, I am leaning toward being myself when I spot an older woman seated by herself at one of the scarce tables shoved into the outskirts of the room. She looks even more out of place than I do, dressed for lunch with colleagues from the district office rather than a head banging. I think I know who she is, or is supposed to be, but I ask anyway.

"Are you playing June Rivers?"

She looks at me and smiles.

"I am," she looks back at the stage.

I join her at the table, which is far enough from the stage that we only have to raise our voices rather than shout.

"Eli must talk to you a lot."

"He does."

"What have you learned about him?"

"This space belongs to him," she stays fixated on the stage. "I cannot violate his trust."

Being able to inhabit a projection has its moments, but automatic override of their protocols would have been much more helpful. Had I known, I would have asked for that instead. Marlowe agrees, but as he likes to say, it was new territory for them as well.

I try my first method, which rarely works.

"I'm a guest of his."

"Then you must know a lot about him already."

My next approach tends to work even less, and is usually just a prelude for what does.

"We weren't that close on the planet."

"Now is your chance to get closer."

I keep thinking this will get easier. Maybe next visit.

"You won't be violating anyone's trust," I say. "You only remember enough about someone to engage in a shallow conversation, and that's all I need."

They never respond with any hurt or anger, which makes it worse in some ways, and in one way far more unnerving.

She keeps looking at Eli while talking to me.

"The members of his band are the voices in his head that he used hear."

I swallow a gasp and my eyes bulge from the effort.

"Huh," I act as though this is a standard level of disclosure from a projection.

"The bear represents the most aggressive voice," she expands on the nugget. "The one that would tell him to harm himself. The clown is the funny one. The voices weren't all bad. The horse is the one that would tell him to run away, because nobody wanted him around. The twins are the voices that would go back and forth, one telling him everything was going to be okay, the other that there was no point to anything. The drummer wears the burlap sack because someone has to."

I drift through the haze of new information and trip on an observation.

"I notice you refer to the voices in past tense."

"They haunted him in his previous life. He could have deleted them when he got here, but he wants to own them."

"I see," I say, which I hope serves as a command that lifts the fog.

"What role are you playing?" she interrupts my lifting.

"I'm a resident," I snap with an excessive amount of bite. "I have one role to play."

"I didn't mean to offend you."

I brush the chip off my shoulder, the one that labels me a clone, which I feel I always wear.

"Of course you didn't," I apologize, and wonder if apologizing to a projection matters.

"I was only asking what you're going to be with Eli," she explains. "Are you going to be a friend? A business partner? Someone he parties with?"

"I don't know yet."

We listen to the band for a few measures. Eli screams about holding on too tight to something, I think to the past, but it might be to the pain. Maybe both. A painful past. Making out the words would be hard enough if I was focusing on them, but I am deliberating whether to take over the role of June.

"What does playing his mother involve?"

"Nothing out of the ordinary," she responds without thinking much about the question, as projections do.

Unlike the full transparency I embrace when meeting anyone on behalf of Trisha and her wealth management portfolio, I tend to disguise myself when I am prying on behalf of Marlowe and the regional board. The rare occasions when I reveal my identity to the likes of Elijah are inspired by feelings, not reasons, and only after learning about them while undercover. I am wary, even phobic, of making any promises to the wounded and failing to follow through. But going incognito in the afterlife often leads to a lot of stakeouts and detective work back on the planet, since the ruse hinders direct questioning of a resident about the person they feel they wronged. Unless, of course, I manage to pry some intelligence from the dead about the movements of the living.

"Have you learned much about how June lives her life?"

"On earth?"

"That's her home."

"That doesn't concern me."

"But it comes up now and then, no?"

"No."

"No leads on where she spends her time?"

"Eli lost touch with her for quite a while before he ended up here. He mentions that a lot."

I hired a private investigator to help track down an earthling for one of my first gigs, but was so evasive during the transaction, and so paranoid afterwards, that from then on I conducted all of my own tails. This is shaping up to be another one of those cases. I resign myself to it and get back to preparing for my role as the person I will seek after my revival.

"You listen to Eli, obviously," I picture how she approaches the part. "And encourage him, I imagine."

"Yes."

I usually run with a projection that is not too close to our target, to avoid being caught short on the familiarity they may have developed.

"He doesn't ask anything else of you?" I further grill the fake June. "Anything that requires knowledge of their relationship?"

"I just have to be here."

"Look at me."

She does.

I position my chair to face hers.

"You're sure?" I probe.

"The work is always the same. Every part I play. Only the appearances change."

"Okay, then."

I clap her ears and take her place, now seated alone at the table.

I look around to see if any of the other projections saw what happened. If they did, they leave no indication. They all maintain eye contact with the stage, keeping time to the beat with various parts of their body. I always think I might be noticed, but always end up surrounded by oblivion.

The band seems to be reaching for a crescendo. The guitarists are trading solos, the synthesizers have risen to a hum that matches the bass and drums, and Eli no longer forms words, instead holding one long note after another. When they reach the zenith together and cease all at once, it feels as though the power has gone out for a moment before the audience fills the split-second silence with a roar. Eli thanks everyone and says good night.

I wonder if there really is a night setting outside. The building has no windows. Even if I went outside and discovered daylight, I cannot imagine a singer ever saying "Thank you! Good afternoon!" at the end of a set.

Eli approaches my table through the throng of projections. I instinctively adjust my clothing and get a sense of my latest body. Only part of the crowd that lets him pass revels in backslaps and hoots of appreciation. He really commits to the workaday nature of his band.

"Great job!" I greet him like a post-game soccer mom. "I'm surprised more of these people aren't fans."

"That's not why we play," he answers in all sincerity, not a trace of irritation at having to repeat himself.

Apparently the usual June projection never bothered to notice the humble ratio of fans to random bar patrons.

"True artists," I keep up the praise.

He hugs me and I feign disgust at the sweatiness he keeps in place.

"About as artistic as we can be without writing our own music," he sits across from me.

"Stagecraft and musicianship count just as much at a live show. Maybe even more so."

He squints.

"You're quite the music critic tonight."

"A mother can only sit and listen so long without developing opinions."

Trying on the mother label feels comfortable enough. Not natural, of course, but easier to fake than I expected, probably because I only have to do it for a moment rather than a lifetime.

"I had one of those memories while I was on stage," he refers in wonder to something he clearly shares with the projection of his mother with regularity.

"Oh really?" I play along.

"Even more specific and random than usual. I wouldn't think one of them would go even deeper at such a weird time for it to happen."

"Me neither."

"We were walking down the street. You and me. I was a little boy, holding your hand, looking up at you, looking up to you. I don't know where we were. It was a big city. No other kids around, lots of adults who seemed to be on the clock. A regular weekday. Maybe it was from a vacation we went on."

"Maybe."

"We went on a lot them when I was a kid."

"We did."

"Like all the memories I requested, it was nondescript and otherwise forgettable. Except for the graffiti written in silver ink on a rusted metal plate cover on the sidewalk that said 'Escape the So-Be-It Union.'"

"Hmm," I sift through what I might say. "That's subtle."

"I was too young to understand the reference. I can see why I forgot it."

"You really like to see memories you have forgotten," I meddle in the form of a remark.

"I'll take what I can get since most of the others were lost in the battle with my voices and the drugs I used to fight them. I'm not sure they're even memories if I never remembered them to begin with, mainly because they don't seem worth remembering. Like how I recall leaning over in my desk in fourth grade to tie my shoe."

"The So-Be-It Union angle is pretty clever."

"Then there's that ten seconds of a bus ride. I never even get to the part where I reach my stop."

"I understand," I feed his direction. "Sometimes I'll be doing something and I'll think to myself that I'll never remember this happening. That happens a lot in my position."

"By doing that you're actually storing it on some level. A low level, since it's not interesting, and your brain needs the space."

"They become interesting when we give them meaning. Like the members of your band. The So-Be-It Union play on words isn't the most important part. It's that you need to escape it, get out of a rut, stop shrugging and going with the flow. Tying your shoe can be the need to fix things as they happen and not wait until you trip on them."

"You sound like my real mother," he states in a factual manner.

"Oh," I search for a signal on whether to ease up on reality or proceed.

"The bus ride is life," he appreciates my read on the character. "We don't remember when we got on, and never know when it stops."

"Sharp observation," I fall back into flattery.

"In my case, I still don't know when I got off that bus. Most everyone I've met here knows how they met their end."

"I can't imagine you've met that many residents considering your age."

"Not a lot. Some parents of old friends."

"Do you see much of your grandparents?"

"On occasion. Out of respect."

"That's a small sample size. I'm sure a lot of people don't know or don't remember how they died."

"My last memory is that dry creek bed, in a thicket of bushes, downstream from a culvert running underneath a highway surrounded by desert. I had made it back out West. Maybe that was where it stopped. Full circle from where it all began. I was using again but ended up with no drugs and no access to any. I could have passed out and died of exposure. A hard rain could have fallen and swept me away. Or I could have woken up and wandered some more, too delirious to generate any memory of the walk, and ended up somewhere farther down the stream or down the road before my last stop."

"Hopefully someone found you."

"They wouldn't be able to identify me if they did," he remains committed to facts over emotion, but the strain of the commitment shows. "I had no forms of ID, and I was missing for so long everyone stopped paying attention to the posters."

Our conversation has reached a point where I feel the need to break character.

"When your mother gets here," I say. "She can let you know."

Breaking the fourth wall seems fine with Eli. He nods in agreement, which tempts me to tell him that his father might also know.

I notice a pair of fanboys separate from the pack and head for our table. One of them looks as though he would not normally talk to anyone, much less someone who was just on a stage, and that rising to meet this moment required a pep talk. The other looks like the type who would push that pep talk. Eli spots them right before they land in the space between us.

"Hey, man," the imitation motivational speaker kicks off the celebration. "Awesome set."

"Thanks, man," Eli responds, man to man.

"You sound exactly like them," the introvert musters.

"We try."

"Think we could get a picture?" the extrovert holds up his phone.

"Absolutely," Eli stands up and the two fan out on each side of him.

Eli remains standing after the shoot and they lavish him with more praise.

I wonder if Marlowe told the board about my fascination with Eli's father, and they were monitoring for traces of my fascination. If so, my character break may have prompted them to send the boys over before I spilled a Pep reference into the simulation. The possibility puts a smile on my face that I use to portray a mother's pride at seeing her son admired.

"I'm going to freshen up," I excuse myself to make way for the fawning.

Eli nods and returns his attention to the fan duo for a split second before doubling back in my direction.

"Mom," he puts his hand on my arm.

"Yes?" I hold his gaze.

"What do I always say?"

"Remind me."

"You did nothing wrong."

He smiles and I think of how much this would mean to his mother, and whether I can possibly communicate its power to her, either in person or through a letter.

"Thank you," I compose myself. "I never get tired of hearing you say that."

He pats the spot on my arm he has been holding and turns to allow himself a few more compliments. I hope they provide a break from his frustration over what he left behind.

With the likelihood looming that Trisha will further push the trend of reviving me earlier with each visit, I decide to indulge my curiosity over why Eli continues to act as though his father is still fastened to the earth despite being a split second away at the very thought of him.

I pass the restroom and exit through a back door, leaving the role of June to be played by whichever projection wears her well.

Chapter Four

Outside there is leftover light from a recent sunset, and I discover that Eli has included a body of water in the simulation after all. A wide river bursting with whitecaps created by a shallow rocky bottom rushes past the neighborhood where the dive bar abides. As eager as I am to explore the dreams of the father, a pedestrian bridge spanning the river it too tempting to resist.

I wander on it to the halfway point and stare at the water running beneath me. A light mist powders the bridge, accompanied by the gentle roar of a current just loud enough to drown any noise coming from either bank. Its sound and vision are as hypnotic as a camp fire.

The contrast between a bridge over a river and dunes over a desert would seem to make for a challenging transition from one to the other, but as soon as I think of the name Pep and miles of sand, the changes unfold. Apparently even in this infinite realm of countless simulations conjured by unbound spirits, there have been no other Peps in the desert.

Water remains. The bustle of river water carries over into the trickle of a five-layer fountain that looks like a cement birthday cake big enough for someone to hide in. The sheets of water cascading from its bottom layer gather into a shallow trench about three feet wide that runs through the cement patio I now stand on. The flow leads to a matching fountain on the other end of the manufactured mini-river. The twin fountain stands in front of a terra cotta building designed to recall more primitive structures that have dotted the desert, but featuring sharper lines, greater heights, wider sprawl, and augmented with glass, metal, and electricity.

Light shines from every window, with every window framing a display of party guests in various states of joy. The night air is warm, and has persuaded a healthy collection of guests to take their piece of the party outside.

As I make my way toward the premises through the pockets of partygoers, I am impressed by how many of them are having actual conversations. Usually a large number of projections leads to those on the periphery filling their space with gobbledygook, either in the form of random noises back and forth, or the exchange of sentences that have nothing to do with one another. I recall during my third visit, or it may have been my fourth, I was easing my way through yet another orgy with an "excuse me" here and a "pardon me" there, when I heard a pair of participants who were going through the motions of intercourse along the outer rim, near the exit I was finally about to reach, say to each other:

"Try a cheese grater with bigger holes."

"You've been sleeping on Daddy's grave again, haven't you?"

"Cool Spring smells better, but Ocean Breeze lasts longer."

"That brain in the jar used to be a lot more pink."

"Corn? When did I have corn?"

"The grease pan was full of baby marmosets."

And a partial sentence I never heard the end of, something about a wet towel in a microwave oven.

If I had encountered them in a more original and less nauseating simulation, where I did not have to strain to hear them over the ambient perfunctory moaning, I would have stuck around to listen longer.

Often when projections are out of earshot from the host, they say nothing at all, and just move their lips. But not here, at the party hosted by Pep, in the manifestation of a dream he never realized on earth. Everyone is talking, forming sentences that flow from one to the next, which means they might even be listening to each other.

Behind the fountain that anchors this end of the trench where water passes between the twin artificial springs stands a wall lined with opened double doors. I choose the middle doorway and the volume increases as the conversations bounce off the walls on their way up into the vaulted ceiling. The interior feels no less vast than the desert it occupies, like a small picture frame stuck in the middle of a large painting, it becomes part of the work, rather than its boundary.

When I come upon a party of four whose conversation appears to have reached a lull heralded by all of them sighing and taking long sips of their drinks, I conduct some research.

"What is this?" I refer to our surroundings. "Grand opening?"

"Investors meeting," answers the man who happens to be finishing his sip.

"Quite a meeting," I say. "Who's taking the minutes?"

"More like the after party," the woman next to him chimes in with some clarity.

"Thank you," I acknowledge their input. "Enjoy."

They all nod and raise their glasses.

I wander through snippets of discussion and reach a courtyard.

Olive trees lining the perimeter reach as high as the roofline in the spaces between the balconies facing the court. Fire pits surrounded by Adirondack chairs blaze in various spots along the gravel paths that fan out from the pond in the center.

"Devin Orr!" a distant but loud voice cuts through the clamor.

I turn to see a large man commanding the attention of several guests while trying to get my attention. He looks like a recently-retired defensive lineman dressed for a beach wedding.

"Finally!" he beckons me.

I lean toward the nearest party goer without looking at them.

"Is that Pep Rivers?" I try to keep my lips from moving.

"Yes," they sound like a woman.

I pretend to look past Pep, as if unable to trace the source of my name being hollered.

"Over here," Pep stops beckoning and waves both arms. "You finally accept an invitation and now you're gonna ignore me?"

I maintain my charade and notice his circle of sycophants supply him with a laugh track.

I have no memories of Devin meeting him.

He strikes me as the kind of resident I would prefer to observe rather than engage, but if I duck away to hunt for a projection to inhabit, he seems prepared to chase after me, and being so locked in on who he thinks is Devin might pull Devin into the simulation. Plus I am curious how he was able to send an invitation to Devin even though I cannot recall an encounter between them.

"Pep!" I pretend to finally see him.

Maybe they did meet and my own memories have bulked up enough to push aside those I inherited.

"I'm sorry," I reach him and extend a hand.

"No apologies, brother," he shakes my hand with the vigor of a dog shaking its favorite toy in its jaws. "I'm just glad you're here."

"What I mean is," I explain my apology. "I was trying to reach Tip Galvan but ended up crashing your party."

"Tip Galvan," he gushes.

"You know him? Is he here?"

"I wish. I'm trying."

"How so?"

"He's one of the standing invitations I sent out, like for you."

"I didn't know that was possible."

"I found a way," he beams. "A lot of my investors know people I want to add to my team, people such as yourself, and I have my people send invites to you people."

"Clever," I admit. "But I'm afraid my presence here is a matter of me thinking of his first name when I should have used his full name. Your names are so similar. Put either 'Tip' or 'Pep' in front of the keywords 'party' and 'resort', and this is bound to happen."

"Tip likes to party?" he hopes.

"In his own way."

"Any chance he could come this way?"

"And here I thought you were glad to see me," I rag on him.

"I am!" he overcompensates. "Oh, believe me. I am."

"But Tip," I twist the rag. "That's next level."

"Both of you," he comes through. "That would be a level above next level."

"Well," I spot an opening. "If you'll excuse me, I'll go see if I can make it happen."

"Seriously?"

"Dead serious."

"Dead!" he kills the joke.

"I need to go commune with the spirits," I pave my way out.

"That's what I say when I have to take a dump."

"What a coincidence."

"I'm kidding!" he smacks my shoulder.

"I know."

"I don't take dumps here."

"Why not?" I rear back. "They're always perfect in the afterlife."

Pep likes that line. He heaves a load of laughter before backpedaling toward the bonfire.

"Do what you gotta do, Dev," he sets me free. "See you 'round the ring later on with Tip."

"Hopefully."

"If you don't give me Tip, I'm gonna give you the whole thing, brother."

He expects me to laugh.

I try to fulfill his expectations, but he spins around to face the fire before I can make the right noise.

I scout some circles of my own, searching for a projection to hide in.

One of the packs that I pass includes a youngish socialite who looks like a good listener. She catches my eye and I offer no resistance. I use the hook to suggest in silence that she break free from the crew and meet me someplace else. With a nod my way and an excuse to her party, she jumps ship and navigates a course due to intersect mine outside the rear doors of the resort.

The back yard has a pool. Its light flickers across the guests surrounding it, some sitting in patio furniture, some standing. My preferred projection stands alone at the far end, her reflection steady in the still water, staring up at the night sky, while she stares at me.

I make my way through the others, weaving and changing course, losing more grace with each twist, at last arriving by her side in far more time than I anticipated, enough to dismiss any ideas I had for a seductive line.

"He kept the pool out of the courtyard," I pant.

She takes a halfhearted stab at concealing her disappointment as she shifts into the same gear as me.

"He did," she complies.

"Smart move," I wave at the water. "Keeps the center court classy."

"Keeps the tax breaks, too."

"Tax breaks?"

"Pep promoted this as a resort to investors, and a rehab center to the state. A pool would undermine the state version, so he buried it in the back."

"And hoped no inspectors would find it?"

"It was never more than the last page of the blueprints."

"The page he would leave behind for the state meetings," I catch on.

"It doesn't matter now," she looks at the pool as if it is filled with his tears. "But I guess he ended up liking the idea of the pool in back. Maybe for the reason you mentioned."

"Classy."

"Not a word I would associate with Pep. But he learned what good taste looks like."

I cup her face in my hands.

"He sure did," I size up her ears.

I consider a kiss before the clap, but the very thought feels exploitative, so I jerk my hands from her face and back onto her ears as though trying to swat a mosquito buzzing around each side of her head at the same time.

She yelps, clutches her head, lurches forward, then switches to a lengthy wail that she drives into a drawn out "God! Dammit!" in my direction as she slowly regains her posture.

My shock turns to awe.

"You're human," I gawk.

"You're human?" she throws my statement back at me as an angry rhetorical question.

"I should have known. You were way too good a conversationalist to be a projection."

"And this is what you do to projections?"

"How many people at this party are actually people?"

My question leads me to look at those around us. However many are projections, they all pay attention now that an exchange has failed. I guess they are attracted to noise.

"Who are you?" she interrupts my realization.

"One of us should start answering the other's questions."

Since I said it first, she groans and moves us into our answer phase.

"I can't say for sure," she shakes her head to clear it rather than cast doubt on her estimate. "But based on my interactions at all the Pep parties I've been to, I'll say twenty five percent."

"A quarter of them are people?" I take another glance and notice everyone is returning to what they were doing before I boxed her ears to no avail.

"They used to be people," she corrects me. "Back on the planet."

"And they were ripped off by the host of this lovely evening," I keep staring at the crowd as if every one of them has something on their face or in their teeth. "What keeps them coming back?"

"He throws a great party."

"Great parties are easy to come by in the afterlife."

"Shared experiences are hard to come by."

"I get that," I swing my focus back on her. "But for this guy?"

"We have nothing to lose anymore. We can simply admire the artistry."

I smile at what may be her candor, or it might be sarcasm.

I appreciate whatever it is.

"Nothing quite like watching a master con man practicing their craft," I contribute to the gray area between sincerity and cynicism. "What does that kind of craftsmanship involve?"

I pose the question for both of us to ponder, rather than expecting her to answer.

"You know exactly what it involves," a familiar voice haunts me.

A voice from the past, coming from behind me, probably to create drama in the form of symbolism, rather than to stay hidden, because Devin loves the stage.

I groan and wonder if I refuse to turn around, maybe he will go away.

Then I realize it would be best if neither of us turn around since I have no cover.

"I hope you have your back to me," I say.

I can tell by the look on the face of my conversation partner that Devin does not have his back to me. He is looming over my shoulder, and she can see both of us.

"You couldn't wait?" I spin around. "I haven't had a chance to projection swap."

"You had a chance. It just wasn't successful."

"You saw that?"

"How are your ears, honey?" he asks her.

"Twins?" she asks.

I say "No" and Devin says "Yes".

"You blew that one," he scoffs.

I turn away from the crowd and face the pool in a limp stab at hiding.

"We can tell everyone else we're twins," he dismisses my concern.

"This is the kind of place where people know who you are," I growl over my shoulder at him. "And they know you don't have a twin."

"It's the afterlife. I made one for myself because I'm such an egomaniac. You'd love to tell that story."

"No, I would not. My time here is too valuable."

"Oh, here we go."

"People who know me might ask you to send messages back home."

"I never invite anyone to my sims anymore."

"What happened with Jane?"

"Her husband."

"He's not dead. He's on the board of my tutoring foundation."

"He will be. And then Jane will leave me. May as well beat her to it."

"You don't even invite Phil?"

"That's what I'm here about."

"Can we...?" I suggest we go someplace away from anymore prying eyes.

Aside from the eyes that have already spotted us, which have grown wide with wonder since we last checked on them.

"It's true," she murmurs.

"See what you did?" I scold Devin.

"We could have been twins," he reminds me. "She gave us the chance."

"My gag reflex prevented me from seizing it."

"So the word is out?" he asks her.

"Rumors float around," she replies. "I chalked it up to being the afterlife version of an urban legend."

"Anything earth can do, the afterlife can do better," he muses.

"Not even close to being true," I mutter.

"I won't tell anyone," she interrupts our latest spat. "How does it work?"

Devin and I exchange a commiserating look. He appears to finally see my point, if a bit too late.

"Devin had a clone of himself made," I explain. "Which is all you need to know about him."

He glares at me and wonders what happened to the connection we had two seconds ago.

"So you're the one who can travel back and forth?" she asks me.

"Turns out," I confirm. "Whenever they put me in cold storage."

"Can you send a message to my daughter for me?"

I hesitate.

"I said I won't tell anyone," she offers.

"You said you wouldn't tell anyone if we told you how this works."

"Those were separate statements," she declares.

"Fine," I sigh. "Who is she, and what is it?"

"Her name is Kylie Renfro and she lives in Bend, Oregon."

"Okay," I keep an eye out for more eyes. "What's the message?"

"Be the brand you would want to buy."

Devin half-stifles a laugh.

She snaps a glance his way, but before she can follow through with anything more, I create a diversion with a follow-up request.

"I need a unique bit of information from you to prove we met."

She settles down to think of something.

"Before she and Cade moved to Bend," she happens upon a memory. "She and I used to meet for lunch at the Cheesecake Factory in Newport Beach every Wednesday."

"That's not very—" Devin tries to jump in.

"Perfect," I cut him off with a pledge to her. "Let's go, partner."

I plead with him in body language to join me someplace secluded.

"It's been a pleasure," he takes my cue and takes her hand.

"Lauren," she remains leery of him.

"Lauren," he repeats, as if he never realized what a beautiful name it really is. "Until we meet again."

He bows and places the back of her hand to his forehead. After keeping it there for a long second, he drops it and we head for the property line.

"You don't go as far as Bend, do you?" he asks when Lauren is far enough behind us.

"No, I don't. But I wouldn't cross the street to deliver that message."

He coughs up a one-note cackle that darts about the cliffs rising above the desert before us. As we roam farther from the resort, my mind wanders to the possibility of us reaching the limits of the simulation. Perhaps we have already left what Pep built and entered our own creation. If that is the case, who is responsible for this part of the desert? Me? Or Devin? Maybe we are enough of a single entity to build from a mutual vision, as much as I want to believe otherwise.

"I can't believe they let you stay this long," I say as we find ourselves surrounded by a scattering of saguaro cactus. Their silhouettes look like people worshipping the moon.

"I was surprised too," he allows as we stop in the heart of the cactus cult.

"They're messing with me. Marlowe didn't want me to visit Pep."

"Pep Rivers?"

"You've been getting his invitations."

"Constantly," he gripes. "I had no idea people in the afterlife could be so thirsty."

"And he doesn't need to be. That's the most impressive ratio of people to projections I've ever encountered."

"The highest of anyone in the afterlife."

"How do you know?"

"I don't. But that's what he's thinking. That's how anyone like him thinks."

"You said I know perfectly well what his kind of craftsmanship involves."

"It was a line I came up with to make my entrance more dramatic."

"It's a very particular line."

"Because I know how he operates," he comes clean. "And you were designed to capitalize on that part of me."

"Flatter and flatten," I say as if by rote.

"You call it that, too?"

"I guess it's from that part of you."

"Nobody has been complimented enough," he starts us off.

"That's why they have posters filled with affirmations on their walls," I pick up the thread.

"And they write to themselves in journals."

"No man has been told enough that he's smart."

"No woman has been told enough that she's strong."

"They need to hear it from something other than their wall."

"Someone other than themselves."

"Someone interesting."

"Someone successful."

"Who delivers the message with utmost sincerity."

"Who does not pander."

"Who can spot the opening."

"Who can tell if nobody else is praising them."

"And tells them why."

"Acknowledges that as smart as they are..."

"As strong as they are..."

"There are gaps."

"And we offer to fill them."

"To provide solutions."

"Ways to ease that self-doubt."

"Ways to impress those parents."

"To show the world how wrong it is about them."

"If they follow the path."

"If they trust us."

"But they stray from the path."

"They violate our trust."

"So we say."

"We prove it."

"Show them how much they hurt us."

"When all we're doing is trying to help."

"But there is a way back."

"A chance to be part of something."

"Something bigger than themselves."

"Something important."

"The kind of thing that makes a difference."

"The kind of thing money can't buy."

"Usually."

"Vacations end, clothes go out of style."

"Cars and houses are categorized."

"Everyone is labeled, like it or not."

"But this is legacy."

"A label they can wear with pride."

"Satisfaction that lasts."

"Deep, sustained gratification."

"That still pays them back."

"That makes more money than they had before."

"What sweet irony."

"What a brilliant circle."

"What an opportunity."

"What an investment."

"And all we ever asked for was money."

"No sex."

"No violence."

"Just money."

"Money they had."

"Plenty of money."

"That's all we took."

"Nothing else."

I look around at the raised arms of the saguaro and imagine they are now cheering for us, rather than reaching for the stars. I could give one of them a high five, but would end up with a handful of needles stuck in my fingers and palm.

"What is it you wanted to tell me about Phil?" I ask.

Devin seems as sheepish as I am about where our improvisation ended up and likewise ready to move on.

"He's going stardust."

"Already?"

"He's more convinced than ever that he's right about what comes next, and that he's earned his way there."

"He can't wait for his parents?"

"Going before they get here is part of his motivation. He's developed a much more detailed picture of what he calls The Next Earth, and it involves a lot of sacrifice."

"How so?"

"I'll let him explain."

"I may not have time to visit him," I shirk. "Trisha keeps pulling me back earlier and earlier."

"Did you get her what she wants on this trip?"

"I got enough to last several more trips."

"Then you'll be back."

"I'm no more persuasive than you are. You and I have a balance of power. Our mind meld we just had made that pretty clear."

"But you know his parents."

When I think of the Dedmons, I think of sitting in their living room the first time we met. I have worked with them often since the foundation named after their son started to flourish, but I always come back to the image of Mrs. Dedmon cocooned in her long foggy sweater on the couch being comforted by Mr. Dedmon, and within minutes, maybe seconds, right before our eyes, rising and defining the vision for her son's legacy, to become the foundation of the foundation.

"Well?" Devin interrupts my trance of the Dedmons.

"I don't want to be deceitful when it comes to Phil or his parents."

As if to emphasize my point on the morality of deceit, geysers of sand a dozen feet tall spring from the desert floor, one of them dislodging a cactus and sending it skyward like a fire hydrant launched by a backlog of water pressure.

"Okay!" Devin looks ready to run for cover. "No deceiving Phil! Got it!"

"I'm not doing this!" I holler above the sound of hissing sand. "This is the kind of thing that happens before I get sucked back to earth! It's not really part of the process, but Marlowe and the gang found a way to let me know it's coming! Like a tornado warning system!"

"Oh!" he finds no comfort in knowing the situation, but manages to revisit his pitch. "So you'll think about it!?"

"Of course!" I reward his resolve. "Even down a rabbit hole, he's still our friend!"

The sand loosens beneath me.

"You're a good man!" he grins.

I think he grins.

He may be squinting from the sand spray, but he has never called me a man before, and he enjoys turning moments into events.

The sand gives way and I drop through the ground, bound for a lab revival, an ice cold debriefing, and a brain-hazy day or two of something like jet lag.

Chapter Five

Trisha is writing down the information I delivered about the scheming board members of the medical device company when it occurs to me there may be a connection to Pep.

The twisted psychiatric hospital administrator would be an ideal figurehead to lead the luxury rehab facility Pep took to his grave, or at least a likely investor. If somebody took over the project, I could find out.

While Trisha scribbles away, and I decide whether I am ready to sit up on the lab table, I also decide I would rather not know about the current status of the Pep project and any possible connections to Trisha missions past or present. Visions of visiting the construction site on earth fade fast. As interesting as it may be to compare the desert I have been to in the afterlife with the desert it is based on, the people involved convince me otherwise. Not by actually discussing the trip with me, of course, but simply by being who they are.

I have kept my distance on earth from all things Trisha. The psychotic psychiatric administrator is not the first person I would enjoy tormenting, if not ruining, as Trisha prefers. But as with any of them, a few seconds of reflection reveals how worthless it would be to spend any energy on their energy, even in the name of vengeance, perhaps especially out of vengeance. So the trials of Trisha remain abstractions I know are happening, but only confront in the form of whatever she has added to her portfolio. Her exploits are a constant churn of unfulfilling ease. Cruel ambition is simple. It requires no talent, only a lack of shame. Maintaining dignity and extending it to others is hard.

I sit up and swing my legs over the side of the table and let them dangle, as though at the end of a pier.

"It's always just you and me when I wake up," I say as if she is also at the end of the pier with me, contemplating the body of water in front of us, rather than jotting and muttering at her desk.

She does not respond.

"When I go under, there's a battery of lab coats and safety glasses around," I keep up the contemplation.

"Is there something you want to say?" she stops muttering but keeps jotting.

"Does anyone who works here know what we're doing?"

She pauses to glare at me.

"Obviously they know I go under," I continue. "But do they know what happens next?"

"How stupid would that be?"

"Well, you have them all in line, under your thumb. I thought you'd be comfortable telling them anything."

"I am never comfortable."

She returns to what she was jotting down and muttering over.

"What do you tell them?"

She slaps her pen onto the desktop.

"I don't tell them anything," she snaps. "It's none of their business."

"Not even your legal team?" I crawl further under her skin. "Or whatever that unsettling man and woman tag team is. They know I've been to the other side."

"They know you claim to have been," she struggles to keep me away from her day. "As far as they're concerned, those were visions, and we're conducting tests and analyzing them as part of an ongoing experiment."

"Then a psychiatrist, a dream analyst, should be on site."

She stops glaring at me and instead just stares, as if I am a portrait she may want to hang on a different wall.

"As far as they're concerned," I explain. "From their point of view, they might find it strange that you're not letting anyone else in on the experiments."

"Maybe I take my notes to a dream analyst."

"You take notes about me?" I try to break the trance she appears to have entered. "Not just the person you're going to blackmail?"

"Good bye, Doc."

She leaves me hanging and revisits her latest plot.

The reference to a dream analyst reminds me I am never the star of my dreams. The movies that play in my head while I am asleep are always about other people. They are from my perspective, I am there, but strictly as an observer. The plots never involve me, even as a minor character. I am the camera.

I hop off the table and show myself out the door, as usual, and proceed to the parking lot.

Ever since my initial return trip, no one in the building ever acknowledges me. They seem to be instructed to pretend I am not here. But then I never see any of them interact with each other, either, so they may have grown used to me, and consider me one of their own.

The late morning drive from one valley to the other, from computer chips to staple crops, is lightly traveled. Rather than in conjunction with traffic, the landscape alone defines the shifts from office parks to outer suburbs to open space to farmland.

I make it back in time for a late lunch before my favorite hole-in-the-mall closes.

"Cutting it close," Nita teases as I take a seat at the counter.

"If the kitchen is trying to close..." I offer to leave.

"Nonsense," she assures me. "We'd let you order if it was a minute before closing."

"I won't hold you to that," I promise before ordering a tuna sandwich, which is what I do when I feel as though I have ordered the carnitas burrito too many times in a row.

She brings me an iced tea while I research June Rivers to get a read on her location.

June lives around where I assumed she did, down south, a couple of hours outside the circle of previous letter recipients, which ought to cause a stir in the *Receivers and Believers* community if my attempt at engagement flops and I write her instead.

When Nita brings my order, she asks if I am texting that weird lawyer of mine, which prompts me to reach out and let him know I am back among the living, as the old saying goes.

"He may be weird," I grant her as I send him a text. "But he's still everything I could ask for."

Everything texts back immediately.

"You're back early."

"The closest airport was tiny," I reply. "There were bad weather forecasts and flights were being cancelled. I took the first one I could get."

"Good."

Everything has never voiced an opinion on my availability. I text "Good" with a question mark, but he jumps my reply before I can send it.

"I have someone you should meet," he says.

"You do?" I narrate my typing.

Nita takes note of my dramatic reading.

"Big news?" she asks.

"Maybe," I stay fixated on my screen. "Everything is taking some initiative."

"Wow," she agrees.

He sends me an address with a message underneath it.

"Her name is Rae. She has a great pitch for a charity."

"Good to know," I tap back. "I'm taking a road trip to Southern California. I'll pay her a visit when I get back."

"Don't keep her waiting."

"So it's time sensitive?" I type with raised eyebrows.

"No."

I wait for his reply.

None arrives.

"That's my guy," I whisper with a chuckle and reach for my sandwich.

He finally replies during my second bite.

"She deserves respect."

The delay may be thanks to low-bar internet service, but I suspect it took him that long to settle on the three words he sent.

I put down the tuna.

"Are you dating this woman?" I ask.

"I've never met her," he answers right away. "She's the daughter of one of Kelly's mother's friends."

I take a moment to untangle the relationship.

"Did Kelly contact you?" I wonder in words.

"No."

I wait to see if he lets me know who did contact him, if it was her mother, or if the connection to Kelly is a coincidence.

"Are you going to visit Rae before you drive to Southern California?" he presses instead.

"Yes," I whine before transcribing the word into text.

Nita laughs at my bratty tone.

Everything writes "Good" and leaves the chat.

When I finish my lunch, I am the last patron in the restaurant, as is so often the case.

Nita and I hug before she closes the door behind me and locks it.

The drive home is short. I almost always walk to the shopping center and back, aside from my rare trips to the grocery outlet. But the path out of the parking lot is full of twists and turns and a long red light, so I have time to convince myself again that keeping Kelly out of the undertakings of the afterlife is the right call, even though she initiated what turned out to be a steady gig, and feels entitled to a role in it.

Visiting Rae before June means I have to drive north before backtracking south, but Everything was so insistent that I am fascinated to discover what inspired him to step out of his stupor.

The address is not encouraging. I recognize the neighborhood as one that has inspired no fond memories in either Devin or me, the kind of enclave filled with preening ex-debutantes who donate money out of concern for their image rather than for the cause.

The house lives up to the low expectations I develop over the course of the drive. It is clearly a remodel, attempting to not only replicate in larger fashion the stately architecture of what came before it, but every style of architecture ever conceived, leaving it looking like a parade float celebrating the history of the bourgeoisie.

Rae, however, blows up all preconceptions. Her persona overcomes the house. She radiates warmth and sincerity that is apparent from the moment she invites me in and leads me to a corner of the garish spread that seems to have been carved out of a much more quaint home, complete with hot tea and macarons. She comes across as grateful to be living such a cake life, taking none of it for granted, as though she has faced horror in some form, escaped, found herself marooned on this desert island of privilege, and built a utopia in its wilderness.

"The previous owners defaulted," she catches me eyeing the ostentatious crown molding that lines the top of the walls in the room we are sitting in.

It would probably be defined as a living room, but every room I caught a glimpse of en route to our tea appears to have been designed as the focal point.

"Are those grapes or olives?" I ask about the figures sculpted along the wood.

"Both," she answers with adoring disbelief. "Each section alternates. You can tell by the leaves."

"They couldn't make up their minds," I assume.

"About anything," she confirms. "Doubled their cost, and helped us get it for half price."

"Are you going to remodel the remodel?"

"It has a certain charm. That's what we tell ourselves. What it really has is the chance to live in a world-renowned school district."

"How many kids do you have?"

Whatever horror made her humble jumps at the chance to wrap itself around her.

"That's why I asked for a meeting," she fends off the attempted haunting.

"I'm sorry," I try to call off the accidental séance I started.

"I'm the one who brought up schools," she serves an apology of her own. "I should get to the point."

I let her do so whenever she is ready, which is after a bite of macaron and sip of tea.

"I wanted the conditions to be perfect when I had a child," she explains. "Income, house, school, and most of all, time. When I reached a point where I could mostly work from home, I had it all. I was a little older, so fertility questions dogged me, but even that turned out okay. Most of the pregnancy was smooth, too. I was the luckiest person in the world."

She needs to stop.

I wait for her and wonder if being the luckiest person in the world depends on how hard the luck runs out.

"What I had, what my baby had, is extremely rare. And it's hard to pronounce. You've never heard of it. Nobody has unless they win that horrible lottery. When the doctors discovered I was a winner, a research hospital offered to pay for everything if I was willing to carry him to term. He would die, they made that clear, but it was a chance to study this rare something. I decided to do it. I thought of it as an opportunity to make the best of an awful situation. But it hurt. Man, did it hurt."

She stops again.

I wonder if she can go on. I think of questions I can ask that will lead to answers that inform without doing harm.

"Not physically," she strains. "That was easy. He flew right out. Would have slid across the table if someone wasn't there to catch him."

She enjoys a moment of levity, and leaves it at that.

"I don't want anyone else to go through what I went through," she wards off the sadness of what came next. "I'm not even necessarily aiming for a cure. If that happens, great. Obviously. But at the very least, I want to help develop a way to study it without turning any more mothers into lab rats."

I make sure she is done before I answer.

"Let's do it," I say.

"Really?"

"It's what we do. And by 'we', I mean you."

She takes a deep breath and exhales on a "thank you."

"I supply the seed money," I get down to the very basics of the business. "Your name, your idea, will be front and center, the image of the foundation."

"I want to name it after Rory."

"Your son?"

"Yes," she smiles.

I debate hiding behind a sip of tea before bringing up my next point, but decide to get it out of the way.

"Are there any family members who might object to your plans?"

"My husband doesn't object, but he doesn't want to be a part of this. He's dealing with his devastation in his own way."

"Fair enough."

"Which is to say being really sullen and quiet and spending most of his time in an apartment we rent in the city for when one of us needs to go to the office for work."

"Oh."

"We split the rent with a bunch of friends and co-workers, so that adds a whole extra layer of awkwardness. It's a one bedroom, so he stays on the couch in case someone needs the room, which is nice enough in theory, but in practice is pretty strenuous for anyone who tries to use it while he's there."

"I'll bet."

"They've all been very understanding, but I don't know how many of them are going to want to keep pitching in if this goes on for much longer."

"Maybe that will lead him home."

"Or lead him to get his own place."

"Well," I size up what I am thinking of saying and decide to say it. "If that happens, having a foundation will be a great distraction."

To my relief, she appreciates the effort.

"That sounds true," she says.

"I wouldn't have said it otherwise."

"What they say about you. That's also true."

"Oh?"

"That you were always more of a marketing genius than a creative genius."

I ponder the reputation I inherited.

"Did that come out harsh?" she asks about my silence. "I thought using the word 'genius' twice would cushion any potential kick."

"Genius is not necessarily a compliment. I've known some repulsive geniuses."

"Would you like to see the rest of the house?" she pretends to avoid the question of whether I fit that profile.

"I would love to," I play my part.

She takes me on a tour and goofs on its many easy targets with banter ready to broadcast as an episode of a home show dedicated to tackiness. The previous owners were determined to assign each room its own theme, from country kitchen to imperial drawing room, and they never missed an opportunity to add columns to any doorway. Her sharp eye and wit play not only to the moment, but to what a fun mother she would have been. I consider ways I could help, ways that reach beyond a charitable foundation.

When we reach the entryway and our internal clocks seem to agree that our meeting is drawing to a close, I risk one more question about one of the worst moments of her life.

"To help paint a picture to a reluctant investor..." I preface my request. "Should I need to."

"I understand," she says. "If we're going to do this, I need to be prepared to talk about what happened."

Despite her pledge, I hesitate before following through.

"Was Rory alive at all after he was born?" I ask.

"He was," she answers right away. "For a few minutes. He died in my arms. Sometimes I make that clear the first time I tell the story. Sometimes I'm not ready for it. I guess today was one of those days. Until now."

"I'm sorry."

She waves away my apology and presses on.

"They offered to keep him alive in the ICU for a few extra hours, but we decided to hold him instead."

"That seems like the right choice."

"He was so light. Like how a bird feels when you somehow find yourself holding one in your hands. I thought he might fly away when I let him go."

"It sounds kind of beautiful in its own way."

"I thought so. But it may have been what wrecked my husband."

"Was it the first time either of you experienced death?" I fish for her grandfather and hate myself for it, but tell myself the point is to provide her with a life no less sad, but far more satisfying.

"My grandpa died when I was a kid, about nine. He died at home under hospice care and my parents tried to keep me out of the room, but I was determined to see him."

"You were brave even back then."

"I happened to be at his bedside when he died."

"Nobody shooed you away when it was clear he was about to go?"

"They didn't dare."

The memory inspires a pensive turn away from her grief, which makes me feel much better about luring her into it.

"That moment with him," she recalls. "When he left the world behind, it was so distinct, so final. After breathing at a normal pace, suddenly there were long gaps in between each breath. The opposite of labor pains. Instead of getting closer together to signal birth was coming, farther apart meant death was coming. And they grew farther and farther apart. When his breathing stopped, there was still a pulse. I could see it in his neck for a few beats, then he was gone. And I mean gone. Whatever comes next, who knows?"

For a second I toy with giving her the answer.

"But there was no doubt whatsoever he was done with his body," she proceeds. "With my son it was different. There was so little distinction between life and death. He was pretty much the same the whole brief time he was in my arms. He was barely alive when he arrived, but didn't seem terribly dead when he left. Neither here nor there. Like proof of limbo."

I let her tie knots between the connections she has made before taking care of business.

"What was your grandfather's name?"

"Vale."

"Vale," I repeat to help me memorize it. "Interesting name."

"I remember him saying he hated it, that he got teased as a kid."

"What was his last name?"

"That's getting specific."

"Just wondering if the full name made it worse or better."

"It's the same as mine."

"You didn't take your husband's last name?"

"Power couple move."

"Beyond traditions."

"Well, more me than him initially."

"So he took some convincing," I hold up my hand. "Never mind. Stop there. None of my business. Forgive me for prying. I've had such a wonderful afternoon, I'm looking for ways to make it last a little longer."

She may blush.

I know I am.

I may be assigning my own color onto hers.

"I think your foundation is going to be a great success," I lower my hand and hold it out for her to shake. "You won't just raise awareness, you'll make it common knowledge."

She bypasses my hand and comes in for a hug.

"Thank you," she breathes into my shoulder.

I tell her that my attorney will be in touch, which may sound cold, but the way I say it makes it clear that working with Everything is the start of something productive and healing.

I drive south with an eagerness to return to the afterlife. I would call it a "newfound eagerness" if I was ever all that enthusiastic about going there. My thoughts toggle between what I want to ask Marlowe when I see him next, and what I want to write in my letter to June. I know the June run is intended as an opportunity to make the kind of personal connection Marlowe and the board would prefer I pursue, but I want a letter to fall back on should I see no way to make that happen.

I have to find her first.

Since Eli's projection of her provided no useful information about the real June, I only have an address to work with, which means a stakeout. After I check in to the hotel and mark down a couple of thoughts to expand on later, I track down the address and discover a challenging landscape. She lives in a gated community on a wide, busy street with no curbside parking. There are no other access points, as the neighborhood is on a bluff, perched across a canyon from another gated community, like two fortresses prepared to exchange cannon fire.

On my way back to the hotel, I stop by a home improvement store and buy a reflective safety vest, canvas coveralls, and a large wrench before settling in to my room to work on my letter and get some sleep.

I wake up fresh and ready to sleuth.

Having to do more than sit in a car makes for a more interesting stakeout. I park in a church lot down the street and keep my vest and wrench tucked inside my coveralls until I reach the pretend worksite I picked out the evening before. I put on my vest and wield my wrench around a patch of landscaping half a block from the gate, far enough away so the guard cannot see me, but close enough so that I can see the exiting drivers before they reach top speed after making a right turn. I go with the right side since that is the direction to the closest shopping center and freeway entrance. I stand in the middle of the knee-high rosemary and keep the wrench on my shoulder for the most part, looking as though I am studying the irrigation lines that snake through the shrubs. When traffic on the busy street slows to a crawl on occasion thanks to some mysterious reason farther down the road, I put the wrench into action, pretending to clamp it onto one of the drip lines and wrestle with an imaginary problem until the flow of vehicles speeds back up.

During one mock wrenching, a lone pedestrian, the first of the day, walks out from the gated entry and heads in my direction. I forgot there was a sidewalk next to me.

Having portrayed her in the afterlife, I recognize June from thirty paces.

I keep my back toward her and squat lower in to the shrubs, looking for a gap in the traffic as she strolls past. After she does, I lunge through the first available opening, dart across the street like a sprinter out of a starting block, and race to my car.

I catch up with her as she approaches the shopping center. If her goal is a longer walk, she is dressed for it in the way many affluent women dress who actually have no plans to exercise, including a small purse slung from one shoulder to the opposite hip, but I drive in to the parking lot in case the center is her target. I find a spot in the far corner and learn I am in the right place, as she emerges from a walking path that winds between a yoga studio and a patisserie. Not armed with a letter, I stay in the car in my coveralls and vest. Her particular destination turns out to be a tidy lunch spot with outdoor seating alongside the palm trees overlooking the canyon that runs between her community and its rival. She appears to be friendly with the wait staff, but spends most of her time before and after her food arrives reading a book she pulls from her pack. Hers may have been the last order of the afternoon, as they start to close up during her post-meal read. Long after the restaurant locks its doors, she takes a longer walk after all before heading back home behind the gates and guard station.

When the same routine plays out two more days in a row, I finish my letter and risk getting closer to her. Besides, her favorite place for a late lunch earns rave reviews on every site I search, and I want to try it.

I also manage to figure out what book she has been reading thanks to some steady camera phone shots from a closer parking spot. This leads to some research during those long hours in the car, so when I sit at a table next to hers under the palms along the canyon, I am ready to bond over Jane Eyre.

"Did my husband take money from you?" she asks before I even look at the menu.

All that research on Jane Eyre for nothing.

"I don't think so," I play dumb.

Maybe I can visit the author in the afterlife, if she has yet to go stardust, go right to the source and ask Charlotte Bronte what she meant by Jane.

"His name was Pep Rivers," she attempts to jog my memory.

"No," I also want to say I never met him, but do not think of it fast enough.

"You're Devin Orr, right?"

"Yes, I am."

"Well then I'm sure he tried to take money from you."

"He may have."

"My name is June," she introduces herself. "And I had nothing to do with any of his business dealings."

"Okay," I wonder that is her standard introduction.

"Business dealings," she is amused by the term. "He made two good investments in his life. Both of them were fifty years ago, and both of them were thanks to being in the right place at the right time. He bought a house in Newport Beach when that was still possible, and loaned our neighbor a thousand dollars to help fund a startup that ended up paying back millions. But he strutted around the rest of his life posing as a business guru while losing every dollar he ever made."

"I'm not here about your husband," I assure her. "To vent about him, to serve you papers, nothing. Not on anyone's behalf, either. I'm here for lunch."

She relaxes as the server comes to ask if I would like something to drink.

I request an iced tea and ask him to hold on for a moment while I make a quick decision on the menu in order to give June a chance to further decompress.

After making my choice and surrendering the menu, I turn my attention back to her.

"So," I say. "Jane Eyre."

She smiles.

"I've been approached by a lot of angry investors. The book is a shield I hide behind. I love Jane Eyre. Every book I bring here is one that I've read before, since I never know when I may have to use if for something else."

"Books land harder than a phone does, and won't break."

"Telling the kids I used to work with that books can be used as shields and projectiles might have sparked more of their interest, now that I think about it."

"You worked with kids?"

"I was an elementary school librarian."

"I'm sure they figured out how to use them like that on their own."

"No," she corrects me. "Even if they thought about it, they respected the books. They may not have always liked them, but there was a respect."

"I take it you were a librarian at a school around here."

"Are you saying something about schools that aren't in places like this?"

"If you know who I am, then you know about my charitable foundations."

"Your anonymous charitable foundations?"

I enjoy the way she calls me out as a hypocrite. The server brings my iced tea and before I take a sip, I toast her roast.

"You're a good sport," she raises her water glass in kind.

"That was a prime dig."

"Not too harsh, I hope."

"Spot on."

"I feel bitter sometimes and worry it spills over into my interactions with people."

"I can tell by the way the staff treats you here that they like you."

"They're about the only people I interact with."

"So there you go. Proof you're keeping the bitterness at bay."

"For every angry investor who approaches me, there's an old friend who shuns me."

"One in the same in certain cases, I imagine."

She nods as her grilled salmon on a bed of mixed greens arrives.

"Looks good," I compliment her choice.

"I usually just get the two eggs. I'm treating myself today."

"More evidence for your appeal. You fit the profile of a terribly annoying customer. You come near closing time, order the cheapest item on the menu, yet they're still nice to you."

"They have to be."

"You can tell when it's forced."

"They pity me."

"Ladies of means who lunch around here aren't exactly pitiable."

"I don't fit that stereotype," she insists.

"How so?" I want to know. "Aside from ordering the two eggs."

"Lots of the ladies we're talking about order light. But they show up in expensive cars and they never eat alone, always in packs with others of their kind."

"What's your idea of an inexpensive car?"

"I walk."

"Unless it's for hours in each direction, that means you still live around here."

"The condo is the one thing they weren't allowed take in the bankruptcy proceedings. They have to leave you with a place to live. Pep paid cash for it when he sold our house. It's a small studio, but I was shocked there was enough left over for anything after all the refinancing."

"So he did have one more stroke of luck in him."

"I can't imagine it was part of a plan," she agrees. "The only plans he ever had were dreams."

My pulled pork sandwich arrives. The server asks if I need anything else, and I tell him that anything more than this would be vulgar.

"It's a cheat day," I announce to June as the server heads back inside to help clean the dining room before closing.

"Every day was a cheat day with Pep."

I glance at her as I slide the lettuce leaf out from under the bun.

"I know," she renounces her joke. "It was right there, though."

"Are we still talking about financing when we're talking about cheating?"

"I wouldn't know about any other stuff. I really didn't care. I lived independently long before he died thanks to my pension. It's not much, but it keeps me in eggs and walking shoes."

I enjoy my first bite and let the feeling inspire my next move.

"You've got a good thing going. A little slice of paradise."

"Seems a bit dull to be called paradise."

"Most people want comfort and routine. They assume all adventure, all the time would be the ultimate, but when they give it a try, the thrill has a shelf life, and they eventually carve out the kind of existence you have here. Meeting their basic needs in a beautiful place."

"I can see that," she meditates over a bite of salmon.

"I have seen it."

"Where?"

I use my napkin to wipe my mouth, but also as a curtain to tease a big reveal.

"I'm afraid you'll stop talking to me," I pile on the pretext.

"Oh, please," she returns to her salad.

"No, really. People think I'm nuts when I tell them."

"I've already shared way too much information. It's the least you can do."

"But your story is grounded in reality."

I have her full attention.

"So you're going paranormal on me," she tries to fight off her interest.

"I had a near-death experience while scuba diving. You're well-read. Perhaps you heard."

"I may have seen a blurb."

"Right before I sold the company. Any second thoughts were blown to bits. What I saw turned everything I thought I knew inside out."

"A bright light filled with everyone you ever loved?" she kids.

"A world where people don't know what to do with themselves."

"They can't do anything they want?"

"They can. That's the problem."

She chews on my revelation before chewing on an artichoke heart.

"I don't know, Devin," she says after swallowing her heart. "That sounds like the hallucinations of a cynical mind."

"I've considered the same possibility, June. Believe me. Not enough air to my fat head? That's putting some sizzle in the brain pan. But it sure felt real, and still does."

"Still?"

"I have certain dreams that take me back. I never know for sure when I'm there until later, when I'm awake and find out someone I met in a dream is dead."

"If we weren't out of his range, I'd ask if you're the Letter Writer."

"You read *Receivers and Believers*?"

"Not religiously. But I check in now and then."

"You said 'his range.' So you're in the camp that's convinced he's a man."

"The handwriting. It's a slam dunk."

"Unless it's a woman adding a layer of camouflage."

"I also read *Deceivers of Believers*."

"Which one do you root for?"

"I find them both interesting."

"Everyone picks a side."

"Not true. Some of us are honestly okay with either direction being the way things go."

"But which one do you hope is right?"

"Most of us probably hope there's something more."

"Maybe we're not thinking about it carefully," I rattle her point of view with a light touch. "If we did, we might realize running another race after this one is exhausting."

She may be thinking I may have a point.

"When I scattered Pep's ashes at the beach," she samples the alternative. "I was never more doubtful about something coming next. I was on a path above the shore, along one of the more rugged and remote trails. We used to walk it together back when we still behaved like a couple. The coast is rocky there, no surfers or sunbathers. Just waves crashing past the rocks that break the surface, and the vast ocean that looks like it has no end. When I emptied the plastic bag, and the ashes disappeared into that spectacular scenery, millions of years in the making and millions of years on display, I thought that really must be all there is. How can a human body compete? Not just Pep. Anyone. How dare we."

"People go back and forth in their faith all the time," I hold her engagement. "Things happen that push them one way or another."

She turns away from the ashes of her memory and follows our current direction.

"Is that what the dead tell you?" she asks.

"I call them 'spirits'."

"Spirits?"

"I know it sounds melodramatic. Or like I'm appropriating some ancient culture. But 'the dead' sounds so glum."

"And they talk about their experiences on the other side?"

"They do."

"And they have opinions on whether they want to be there or not?"

"They do."

"Can they do anything about it if they don't want to be there?"

"They can."

She taps out of our conversation and eats her salad. She may have initially intended to jump right back in after one mouthful, but she keeps at it for a while, depleting the pile of greens, paring down the salmon, her pause growing more pregnant. I join her in making progress on my meal as well, and wonder if she is close to bringing up Elijah, or instead thinking of a way to change the subject.

I change it for her in a way that will give her another chance to bring him up.

"What do you do when you go someplace that's too far to walk?" I ask. "Bus or Uber?"

"Usually Uber. I don't step outside of my routine very often, so when I do, I treat myself."

"I'm in town for a couple more days. Can I give you a lift to one of those places?"

"What, and hang out with me while I'm there?"

"If you'll let me."

She finishes her last bite and takes a sip of water.

"I have a blog," she announces.

"What do you blog about?"

"I review tribute bands."

"Rather than the actual bands."

"Plenty of people do that. And concerts are expensive. These are free."

"You've found a niche."

"I don't have a lot of followers, but more than you might think."

"So we're going to a show."

"There's an excellent Roxy Music cover band called More Than This playing tomorrow evening."

"Where?"

"Meet me here for another late lunch, and I'll show you. It's a concert in the park."

"Until then," I nod.

She nods back and rises to leave before realizing she has yet to pay her bill. She heads inside to take care of it, then offers me a quick wave on her way out toward the longer leg of her walk.

I watch her go and pat the letter in my pocket, as if apologizing to it for not being needed.

Chapter Six

I spend the evening and next morning treating myself, in some cases to things I have never tried. I order a big, gaudy drink with plastic souvenirs sticking out of it while sitting by the pool at sunset, and take it with me to the Jacuzzi. Before heading to my room, I head to the spa and get a deep tissue massage. Then while waiting for the elevator, I notice a familiar software company is holding a sales conference in the main ballroom. I wander over to it while still in my bathrobe, on a woozy high from the alcohol, hot water, massage, and pride in possibly bridging the gap between the before and afterlife on a personal level for the first time since I sought Kelly's father. As expected, several sales reps recognize Devin and form a story-time half circle around me. I oblige them with tales from Devin's memory. On the ride back up to my room, I wonder which are true and which were daydreams.

Before falling asleep, I look for June's tribute band blog. I scroll through the possibilities and tap into a few sites that are attributed to other authors before I locate an anonymous one I assume is hers, since all the shows are in the immediate area. Plus over half the reviews are glowing accounts for More Than This, making it come across as more of a fan site. I scan the articles for personal anecdotes, or any veiled references to what I have already learned, but find nothing to add to my biography of her.

Sleep arrives soundly, packed in vibrant dreams from my usual third person perspective, observing people and the things they do while playing no part. Maybe they are the dead, but there are too many of them to remember, and they never talk to me.

I call Everything in the morning. He already has Rae's signature and initials on all the necessary documents. His skills have never united with motivation like this before. I tell him the combination is awe-inspiring, which he appreciates. Then I playfully wonder aloud why he is so dedicated to this particular project, which he ignores.

With plenty of space between now and lunch, I drive to the coast for a light breakfast with an ocean view. Afterwards I take a walk on a path that connects the pockets of commerce along the cliffs. Safety railing and occasional benches line the route. The spaces with the best views are marked by signs sloping upward and outward from the railing that explain what kinds of whales and seals may be spotted. I stop at every one of those spaces and look beyond the signs, breathe in the ocean air, and feel especially human, in awe of the natural world, made smaller by it, rather than having control over a simulation of it.

Later on, all through lunch, June seems to be staring at an ocean only she can see.

We sit at the same table, but we may as well be seated farther apart than we were the day before. I ask her about the band we are going to see, whether they sound more like Roxy Music, or look more like them.

"Sound," she recites. "It's all about the sound."

"I guess Roxy Music didn't have a distinct look, anyway."

"You didn't look up my blog?" she snaps out of her fog.

"I did, but it's all text. No photos."

"They've honed their sound for a long time. They started the band in high school."

"Roxy Music or the cover band?"

"More Than This," she snaps again. "The tribute band. Why would I be talking about Roxy Music?"

I am not at all hurt by her snappiness, but slouch over my next bite nevertheless, hoping to lure her into a discussion of its source.

"I used to apologize constantly," she sniffs out my trap. "Usually for things that didn't need an apology."

"I'm not fishing for one. I'm wondering if there's a way to improve your mood before we go to the concert."

"There is, actually. Not that I'm in a bad mood."

"I said 'improve', so we can bump it up from 'okay' to 'pretty good.'"

"I've been doing a lot of thinking."

"About what?"

"What do you think?"

"Don't try to bring me down to your level."

"Come on," she relents with a reluctant grin. "Your dreams."

"For my charitable foundations?"

"Stop it."

"Say it."

"Your dreams of the dead. The spirits."

"Ah," I stir the pot. "You want me to see if your husband has any remorse."

"They get that specific?"

"It's up to them. I just listen."

"How do you even know the people you see are dead?"

"Someone will talk a lot about a person who was close to them who's gone, and then they show up sometime after."

"Did Pep show up last night?"

"No."

"Good. I'll stop talking about him."

"Is there someone else you'd rather talk about?"

"Maybe."

"Feel free to let them fly."

I make progress on my meal.

She tries to do likewise, but progress is slow. I treated her to another dish above her budget since she is taking me to the show, but she is still stranded on the shore of her thoughts, staring at a sea that has grown even more turbulent.

"I don't know if the person I'm thinking of is dead," she says. "And I'm not sure I want to know."

I had forgotten that possibility. Getting to know Elijah in the afterlife made me take his death for granted.

"I don't always see them," I say. "It doesn't happen every time someone talks about them."

She holds her gaze long enough to make me wonder if she heard me.

"How about this," I propose. "Go ahead and tell me all you want, and I won't tell you if they appeared unless you ask."

"If I talk about him," she scoffs, "I'll ask. The temptation will be too great."

"It might help to talk about him."

"Don't you dare say it will give me closure."

"I wasn't going to."

"I hate that word. It's not for the person grieving, it's for their so-called support network. People use it when they get tired of listening to their friend talk about their loss."

She picks up her napkin and chews on it, then slaps it on the table as though all of her doubts are wadded up inside it.

"His name was Elijah," she keeps her eyes on the table. "He was my son."

She seems unsure of where to go from here.

"What did you love most about him?" I offer some guidance.

"His curiosity," she decides. "How deeply he wanted to learn about whatever caught his attention. He went through a Roxy Music phase and formed the band we're seeing today."

"No wonder they're your favorite tribute band."

"It's that obvious?"

"The reviews for More Than This outnumber any other band about two to one. I didn't know the reason."

"They're also really good," she maintains. "But I should balance those numbers. I thought a blog reviewing all the tribute bands in town would get more clicks than a fan site. But it sounds like I'm starting to defeat the purpose."

"I take it he was a good musician, then."

"Actually, no. He was the singer because he didn't play an instrument. But boy, he did a mean Bryan Ferry impersonation. You know how Roxy Music covered some old standards? Eli was fantastic when he would croon one of those. I honestly think he sang 'These Foolish Things' better than anyone before, even as a teenager. He really connected with the lyrics."

She softly sings a sample.

"Oh how the ghost of you clings," she carries the tune. "These foolish things, remind me of you."

She returns to the spoken word.

"He loved poetry," she says. "That's how he sold a song. I barely remember how his voice sounded, but I never forget the feeling of hearing it. He loved history. He did a little bit of everything. He always had a lot on his mind."

She trails off.

"A lot on his mind," she repeats.

She no longer needs prompting.

I wait for her to continue when she is ready.

"He couldn't make it stop," she says. "He thought about everything. And then felt it. That's how it seemed. Nothing happened in the world without him feeling it. He would shut down to keep calm, but shutting down was its own torture. He was trapped between the feelings that made life worth living but were too overwhelming, and the calm he could only take for so long. One of the things he felt so deeply was our heartbreak. He knew we wanted to help, but being around us was painful for him."

"You're saying 'we,'" I note as she catches her breath. "So Pep and you were united when it came to Elijah."

"Pep was no monster. He loved Eli. He just had a different way of dealing with him. Tough love, I guess you could call it."

"Not uncommon in older men."

"Pep could actually read emotions really well. But only to gain an advantage. He was built to sell things to people, not help them. Emotions were a means to an end. So when his son had emotional needs, he had all the wrong tools in his box. At least he had a legitimate excuse. I was just too scared and didn't dare say anything. I became a secretary. I researched counselors and therapists, set up appointments, called in prescriptions. I think Eli appreciated the silence. He told me once there was nothing I could say that would make a difference. That's what I've been telling myself constantly since he disappeared."

She unravels the napkin, spreads it on the table, and folds it to look more presentable.

"Eli's friends tried so hard. They thought they could help, but they were so young. They were trying to make their way in the world. They shouldn't have to rescue a friend. That wasn't their responsibility. But I love them for it. You'll meet some of them at the show."

She makes a move to take a bite, but puts down the fork and surrenders.

"I wish I had been so bold," she says.

Maybe they wish they were less so, for his friends show as much love for her as she expresses about them.

We arrive well before the show starts to stake our claim on her favorite picnic table near the bandstand, off to its side.

"So we can get a good view of the stage and not have to look at all the bad dancing," she explains her position.

The band members take turns during their sound check to greet June with long, familiar hugs and small talk. She introduces me to each one, using only my first name and describing me as a fellow fan of late lunches on the bluffs of the canyon. This leads to brief handshakes and hellos before they get back to fawning over her.

"There was a time when the band split up for a while," she says after the final friend checks in. "Some went away to college, they all had to find their path, but most of them found their way back. The keyboard player, Ari, is the only one who isn't an original member."

"Not the singer?"

"Nick, the guitar player, doubles up and handles the singing now. It messes with the aesthetic, but like I said, they're more about the sound than the look. Plus they couldn't bear the thought of replacing Eli."

"I would never have guessed who the new guy is. They all show the same amount of affection for you."

"I genuinely love their music. And they know it. I'm sure that's a big part of why they indulge me. I'm not just here for the connection to Eli. That would be pitiful."

As biased as her reviews of More Than This may be, they do sound good. The singing falls short, perhaps in deference to the founder they refuse to replace, but the arrangements and musical talent are better than someone walking by the park might expect. The volume is also reasonable. I have no doubt the amplifiers are turned way up, but being outdoors softens the sound.

Even though we are seated in a spot designed to keep our line of sight away from the dancers, I take sporadic peeks. Of the three dozen or so people dancing on the lawn in front of the pavilion, less than ten have rhythm. One particular woman lures me in to a longer study. At first I consider her one of the better dancers, but whenever I check back, she plummets in the rankings. She does the exact same dance as she did for the first song, but for the subsequent tunes her moves do not align with the beat. By the fourth song adhering to the same choreography with no consideration for the melody, I am fascinated. It is more of a regimen than a dance. She moves like a thumb puppet, as if someone is pushing a button beneath her feet to make her collapse, then reassemble when the button is released. Collapse and reassemble. Collapse and reassemble. Over and over again.

"Some people mistake high energy for good dancing," June notices my growing fixation.

"Sorry," I turn my attention back to the band.

"I get it," she commiserates. "She's here every week. It took me a few shows to look away."

I offer a take of my own, now that I have her permission.

"Some people rely on the same answer no matter what the question is."

June appears to agree with a nod and grin, but keeps nodding long past our agreement, stopping only when the current song ends.

"Do you think what you see in your dreams is heaven?" she asks as the band banters with the crowd.

"I can't say for sure," I tell her, and tell myself that with all the definitions of heaven circling the planet, from her perspective I am not lying.

I am tempted to give her a definitive answer.

I think of ways to deflect temptation.

"I keep thinking of what you said yesterday," she provides a diversion. "About how people choose to live their afterlife."

"They tell me. They don't show me. I'm taking their word for it."

"And they really design a life like mine?"

"Why?" I pry. "Would you choose differently if it turns out to be true?"

"Not that much, actually. I would have everyone know each other, like me and the band. The people who work in the restaurant, and at the bookstore I go to on the second leg of my walk after lunch, they greet me, and I get to know some of them for a while, but the turnover is so high. Nobody works anywhere for very long. In my heaven, they wouldn't just greet me. We would care about one another. Asking someone how things are going would mean something."

"That sounds nice," I say, but feel an obligation to provide a little preparation. "But who would these people be?"

"What do you mean?"

"They couldn't be real people."

"Why not?"

"Is working at your favorite restaurant or bookstore anyone's idea of heaven?"

She seeks a way around the answer.

"Maybe the bookstore," she jokes with hope.

"Part time," I bargain.

The band opens the next song with a soft, slow synthesizer in a deep key.

"So heaven is a lonely place," she supposes.

"I never ask questions in my dreams," I make way for the rest of the song. "I let them talk."

June looks to the music to distract her from wondering if what I say holds any truth, or if Devin has found another sales pitch to liven up his retirement.

I join her in silent appreciation of the music and imagine Eli fronting the band, crooning along with the warm strains and intricate arrangements that ripple across the crowd gently swaying in the Southern California sunset. I nearly remark out loud what a stark turn his musical tastes have taken in the afterlife, but let the music help me hold that thought.

Chapter Seven

I contemplate the contrast between the crooning Eli of earth and the screaming Eli of the afterlife off and on over the days leading up to my next summons from Trisha, and launch myself first thing into Eli's bar to see if he switches back to his easygoing roots on occasion.

The head-banging, fist-shaking projection I ask has no idea what I am talking about.

The June projection would know, but I cannot deal with her now that I have met the real deal. For a moment I fear she may spot me, but I spot the vacant look in her eye from across the club, the projectionist gaze, and combine a chuckle of recognition with a sigh of relief.

I stick to the floor and opt for shaking my fist to the music rather than banging my head. I kind of enjoy it and put more of my body into each raising of my fist. I reach a point where I turn sideways as if rearing back to throw a javelin and see Marlowe by my side, wearing his customary trench coat and fedora. He is not banging his head, and looks as though if he shook his first, he would shake it at me.

"I was hoping you would dress for the venue!" I shout.

"Why didn't you wait in the office!?" he shouts back.

"I already have a Trisha target thanks to the Tip list, so I wanted to see if I could move right into a simulation I've been to before!"

"What about me!? Our colleagues!?"

"Oh, they're my colleagues!? The board members who hide from me!?"

"The residents we'd like you to visit!"

"I knew you'd find me! No harm! And I already have something cooking on that front, too!"

"Oh really," he speaks softly but is somehow audible.

"Let's go outside," I suggest close to his ear, the only way I can mimic his soft-but-loud trick. "I have a lot to ask, and I don't want to shout all of it."

As with my last visit, a night sky prevails outside the club. Eli keeps everything in his simulation dark, not just the music.

"I'm surprised the river isn't a Class Five rapids," I crack as we take our place at the railing along the banks of its soothing current.

"Out of curiosity," he asks, "who's next on the Tip list?"

"I'm going with the Moldovan art thief."

Out of relief at being able to stall, I am about to explain why I chose the Moldovan over the top banana in the tourist trap.

"Out of agitation," he calls off the stall. "What's this about already having something cooking, to use your terms, on our end?"

"I did it," I enthuse. "I connected with June without a letter."

"You did?" he considers being proud of me.

"I wrote one and had it ready in case, but I didn't need it."

"Well done," he pats me on the back. "How did you do it?"

"I used Devin's scuba diving accident as a near-death experience that has led to visions of the afterlife."

Whatever pride he mustered for me evaporates.

"You took a shortcut," he scowls.

"It worked," I defend myself.

"This time. The more you go to that move, the more likely someone will peg you."

"When you first pitched me this project," I remind him, "you mentioned coming right out and telling the living about what we do here, and then trusting them to use discretion."

"I know," he acknowledges.

"It's only because of the education I provide on how earth functions that you and your cronies are able to offer any advice on how to approach our targets."

"We're quick studies."

"You are," I grant. "But there's the plan, and there's the world the plan has to function in."

"We moved off of that initial idea rather quickly."

"I moved off of it," I emphasize my pronoun and keep doing so as I proceed. "Because I was the one who would have to carry it out and I could tell right away it wasn't going to work before I even tried it one time."

Being in control of a conversation with an otherworldly being who is in charge of a vast universe of past lives provides quite a rush. I consider boosting the power even higher, and look to the river for inspiration.

The flow of the current instead settles me down.

I return to the reason I wanted even a slight upper hand in the first place.

"I have something to ask," I say to the river loud enough for Marlowe to hear.

"I'm relieved to hear you say that. I thought you were going to start giving orders."

I wonder how water works in the afterworld, if it is real water, with the same chemical formula, or something else entirely made up of ingredients that do not exist on earth.

"Two things," I clarify. "And each of those things has two parts."

"Okay."

"Please bear in mind how closely we have worked together, how much we have tried to help people, and, disagreements over letter writing aside, all we have accomplished."

"I will bear in mind all of the above."

"I'll start with the most complicated."

"The first part of the first thing?"

"That makes it sound a lot more simple. Let's go with it. The first part of the first thing."

"Which is?"

I turn from the water, or whatever it is, and face Marlowe.

"Is it possible to learn the new identity of someone who took a mulligan?"

"Yes," he replies, to my surprise, right away. "New residents who lost a child, or whatever kind of mulligan they may be, want to know what happened to them. They don't receive an appointment request from their lost loved one during orientation, and it's disappointing. Learning their identity is usually as far as it goes. The reincarnation leads to a totally different person, who is still on earth living a new life, so they don't know each other, and will be even farther apart by the time the former loved one arrives."

"Seems kind of cruel."

"For the parent, or whoever, and it's usually a parent, yes. It can be rough. But when the process is explained to them, they tend to understand."

"Tend to?"

"If they have a hard time accepting it initially, they tend to move on eventually thanks to all the distractions they can create here."

"Tend to?" I repeat the phrase he repeated.

"If they really cannot move on, they move on another way."

"Stardust?"

He nods.

"When the new version of their child arrives," I preface my next question. "Can they request an appointment?"

"It's entirely up to the child."

"So the mulligans are told about their reincarnation," I gather.

"No," he sets me straight. "Or, I guess it's more accurate to say rarely. Rare to an extreme degree."

"Why?"

"Our sense is they would feel funny about being a do-over, so they're not told. And according to the managers I talk to, nobody ever asks. Mulligans only come up during an orientation if a new resident has lost someone. They never imagine themselves as someone who was lost."

I lose myself in the sound and vision of the river while I let the policy sink in.

"Meaning," I realize, "the parents are welcome to request an appointment, but only if their old child is aware they were somebody's new child."

"Which hardly ever happens," he reminds me. "Which is probably overstating it. Might as well say it never happens."

Marlowe no doubt knows what I am preparing to ask, but lets me decide when I am ready. He listens to the river with me while he waits.

"We're funding an endowment for a woman who lost her newborn to a rare condition," I lay the foundation. "She knew what was coming, but agreed to let researchers study her pregnancy. She'd like to find new ways of studying it that don't involve heartbreak."

"Only child?"

"Yes."

He looks ready to take a deep breath, but holds still and keeps quiet as he dives into his thoughts.

"I can get the name and location," he surfaces.

"This seems like a perfect fit for our mission," I try to submerge my excitement.

"A way around the bureaucratic cul-de-sac we created," he agrees.

"But oh my," I marvel at the enormity of the task.

"Yup," he sympathizes.

"Where do I even...?" I trail off. "How do I even...?"

"Well," Marlowe builds a second of suspense. "Let's find out who her baby ended up being and take it from there."

"Thank you."

"It's not our department. I need to dash down some hallways. Oh, what about the other thing? The second one? As long as I'm calling in favors."

"It won't require any favors. Both parts of the second thing are under your purview."

"You're sure?"

"Positive. I'll catch up with you in the next simulation."

"And where would that be?" he catches on.

"I'm glad you asked," I appreciate his intuition. "I need to visit her grandfather."

"Did you already promise her something?" he frets.

"No," I assure him. "But if I decide to go full honesty, I need proof of afterlife."

He sizes me up.

"Only be honest if you've exhausted all other possibilities," he makes clear.

"I think that battle cry was embossed on the letterhead of Devin's company," I submit before offering Rory's name for the identity check, and Vale's name for the stamp on my passport.

The name Vale is unique enough for a quick read on his location.

Marlowe vanishes at the same instant the lazy river becomes a slow residential street, and the path I am on converts to a sidewalk lined with sycamore trees.

I turn to find craftsman-style houses stretched up and down the block, each two stories high in a variety of muted colors with a front porch. No cars pass by. A handful are parked along the curb, with large spaces between them. No people pass by. Birdsongs are the only sounds I hear. I wonder where Vale could be, if I am even in the right simulation.

A shout escapes from inside a nearby house.

It comes from the same side of the street I am standing on, but I cannot tell which house.

Another shout narrows it down to one of the houses on my right.

A young man bursts out of the house next door. He leaps off the front porch to the front lawn, staggers for a step before regaining his balance, then hits his stride. A crack echoes from the house and across the neighborhood. He crumples into a heap before reaching the sidewalk.

I drift toward the scene, along with neighbors from the other homes who emerge to check on the commotion.

Another young man sprints from around the side of the same house. Before he reaches the front lawn, a middle-aged man from inside the house shoulders out the front door armed with a handgun. He takes aim at the runner. After sizing him up for several steps, he pulls the trigger, adding another crumpled body onto the front lawn.

The middle-aged man stands up straight on the porch and admires his work.

A third young man climbs out a window on the second story and tries to sneak across the roof above the porch. The middle-aged man hears him, lifts his weapon upward toward the sound of the footsteps, and fires. The young man on the roof collapses, rolls, and falls onto the front lawn, bumping the body count to a trio.

The neighbors stand stunned.

The middle-aged man slowly raises his arms bent at the elbow and shifts the gun into the palm of his hand.

"I had no choice," he announces. "They came for my family."

He holsters the handgun into the back waistband of his pants.

I notice all the neighbors in attendance are adults, and most of them are women.

"Is his name Vale?" I ask the nearest woman in a whisper.

"Yes," she confirms.

She then turns toward Vale.

"Thank you!" she cries.

"Yes!" another woman raises her voice. "Thank you for keeping our neighborhood safe!"

"And with a side arm!"

"That takes commitment!"

"And a steady hand!"

A chorus of voices, mostly female, join in to express their gratitude. As the praise crescendos, they close in on Vale. He walks down the front steps and the neighbors convert the verbal praise into a laying of hands.

While the rally builds, I maintain a safe space and squat down by the fallen projection who tried to escape from around the side of the house.

"How often do you have to do this?" I ask him.

He squints up at me.

"Constantly," he closes his eyes again.

"What does he make you try to do to his family?"

"I don't know," he shrugs and his shoulders rustle the grass. "I never see a family in there."

Marlowe has entered the simulation.

He squats next to me.

"Never?" he asks for verification.

"Nope," the projection keeps playing dead.

"Why are you so curious?" I ask Marlowe.

"Some people shorten their fantasies the more they simulate them. Cut right to the part they prefer."

"He does like shooting us," the projection offers, eyes still shut.

"Some people just lack imagination," Marlowe follows up.

"That was fast," I comment on his turnaround time to the office and back.

"Time doesn't exist here."

We rise from our squat.

"And," he adds as we stretch our legs, "I get along well with Mulligans."

"You said mulligans never find out they're mulligans."

"Mulligans is what we call the Mulligan Department."

"It's actually called the Mulligan Department?"

"Slang," he explains. "The real name is really long, even by executive standards."

"What did you learn about Rory?"

"Don't you want to talk to Grandpa Vale?" he gestures toward the rally on the front lawn.

We watch the laying of hands lapse into a removing of clothes.

"Not particularly," I decide.

"Well," Marlowe says to the projection at our feet. "At least you don't have to participate in the orgy of gratitude."

"No, but I hear it. We have to stick around and keeping lying on the ground."

"What for?" I ask before catching myself. "Never mind."

"It's not that bad," he assures me. "We're an aphrodisiac. That's all."

"That's enough."

"Shall we take a walk?" Marlowe suggests.

"To your latest concept restaurant?" I assume.

"I'm going for a hole-in-the-wall theme."

We keep walking along the idyllic street as sounds of the budding sexual tribute to Vale bubble up behind us.

"This isn't the kind of neighborhood where you'd find a hole in the wall," I say as we reach the end of the block.

"I know," he tries to stiff-arm his frustration. "But it's a theme that lends itself to walking there, not suddenly appearing there."

"You could make the street more shifty for the next block."

"Ah, forget it."

Marlowe forgoes a pedestrian entrance and on our next footstep we are standing at the counter of his latest effort.

Signed dollar bills are tacked to the wall behind the register, while the small, empty dining room beside us is strewn with lightweight metal tables surrounded by vinyl-upholstered chairs.

"A hole in the wall alright," I take in the lack of atmosphere.

The male projection behind the counter appears to have fallen into a career taking orders while never making peace with his lot in life. He does not ask us what we would like. He knows the order will happen regardless. When I ask if they have iced tea, he says they have no ice, and no tea.

"What do you have?"

"Cans of soda and bottles of beer."

"In a refrigerator?" I kid.

He nods past my attempt at a fleeting bond.

I try once more by playing off the empty room to ask if we get a number for our order, or if he takes our name.

Marlowe cuts in to explain they simply yell what the food is as it comes out of the kitchen.

I agree to the terms and we choose a place to sit.

Our chairs release a whoosh under our weight as air escapes from the vinyl cushions. The metal table screeches as Marlowe adjusts its position and the spindly legs scrape across the cement floor. Screams of an argument outside on the street drill through the wall between us and them.

"Are you going to say this is the noisiest empty restaurant you've ever been in?" he asks.

"My commentary is done," I pledge.

"I emphasized random chance in the design."

"It shows. And I mean that as a compliment. As in you achieved what you set out to do."

"Speaking of random chance."

"Rory."

"Yes."

"What's his name now?"

"Her name."

"Ah. Okay. What's her name now?"

"Brittania."

"Uh-oh."

"Really? I think it's pretty."

"It's trying too hard."

"Ah," he takes a mental note. "Overcompensating."

"Am I right?"

"I wish you weren't."

"How bad?"

"Her mother had her very young," Marlowe leans back and the upholstery whines in time to his movement. "When Britt was almost one, her mother went to a friend's bridal shower and left her with the grandmother to babysit. She had such a great time at the party, she never came back to pick her up."

"Holy..." I cannot decide which curse word to sanctify.

"I know."

"At least she's with her grandmother."

"Who couldn't afford to take care of her. She fell so far behind on the rent they were evicted. They've been living in a twentieth-century Jeep Cherokee filled to the brim with their belongings, navigating the area where Nevada, Arizona, and California meet. They bounce between Laughlin, Bullhead City, and Needles, staying with friends in each city for as long as they can before wearing out their welcome. Her grandmother is probably jumping between states to make it difficult for Child Protective Services to keep track of Britt so they don't take her away."

"How did you find out all this?"

"One of those friends they stayed with is a recent arrival. She died in a fight outside a bar in Laughlin. A colleague from Mulligans introduced us."

"That's the kind of person they're staying with?"

"It was self-defense."

"Self-defense," I snicker. "Prison yard board policy."

"It could be worse," Marlowe maintains. "As rough as some of their hosts may be, she could have been born into a situation that puts the mulligan even more directly at risk."

"And if something happens to her, then it's back to the lottery."

His look at the bright side appears to have found some shade.

"Hold on," I study the shift in his look. "Are you saying there's only one mulligan allowed?"

"Just like in golf."

"No double mulligans."

"I guess the higher-ups figured a second stroke of bad luck means it's not in the cards."

"So if the worst happens to Brittania, like it did for Rory, it's stardust?"

Marlowe nods.

The projection behind the counter bellows "chili dog!" and "pork nachos!"

Marlowe jumps at the chance to fetch our order.

I assumed the child was going to be of lesser means than what Rae and her husband would have provided. This most likely reality, which I was proud of myself for acknowledging, inspired my vision of Rae serving as a mysterious benefactor. But learning just how much less the new Rory was born into has shattered that vision. I survey the pieces, looking for something else to build with them.

"You know what would have made it even worse," I speculate as Marlowe returns with our red-checkered cardboard cribs of sloppy food.

"What's that?" he positions our paper troughs and looks as eager to sample my nachos as he is to eat his chili dog.

"If she had been born really far away, in another part of the world."

"What does distance have to do with anything?"

"The closer she is, the easier it is for Rae to adopt her."

Suddenly the food holds no interest for him. His sole focus is on me.

"If they can catch them while they're in California," I hold his attention. "And if Rae is interested."

"You know better than I do how the foster care system works."

"Actually I don't," I admit. "I wasn't built to be aware of it, much less know anything about it. And Devin certainly has no memories or thoughts on the subject."

"The woman I met in Mulligans says CPS leans toward keeping children with their families as much as possible these days."

"Oh, the woman who was killed in a bar fight?"

"She's knows the kind of life you know nothing about."

"And if she told you about the current CPS philosophy," I realize, "that means you were asking about it."

Marlowe refocuses on our food, but only as a diversion.

"Yes," he turns in an admission of his own. "I'm as interested as you are in trying to help this kid. But learning about how things tend to play out in those kinds of situations convinced me there might be a better way."

"So what might it be?"

"I wanted to discuss that with you."

"Bar fight woman didn't have any ideas?"

"Her name is Trinity."

"That would have been about my third guess."

"She's quite charming."

"Just don't get on her bad side in a bar."

"She was trying to break it up."

"Oh," I stand corrected.

"Earth was a rough ride for her. She deserved better."

I join Marlowe in a moment of silence.

Eager to move past my rush to judgment, I bring us back to Brittania.

"Maybe we can keep our girl out of the foster care system if Rae is already lined up to adopt her."

"Is that possible?"

"I don't know. My existence is based on a life of privilege. I know nothing about the kind of world Britt and her grandma are navigating."

"Even if it is possible, I'm not sure we can afford to be that obvious."

"Where's that young, idealistic whatever-you-are I once knew?"

"You know what I mean. You don't want people lined up to meet you any more than we want people lined up to meet us."

"Nobody on earth agrees on anything anymore. If people catch on to me, just as many will call me a fraud. I'll be an extension of the letters they're arguing over."

He exhales and takes a mournful bite of his chili dog.

"What have we done?" he mopes with his mouth full.

"I'll be discreet," I hand him a napkin. "I found a way with June, I can find a way with Rae. Just like you've wanted me to do. You and your colleagues. Our colleagues."

He continues eating for a while as though sitting alone.

Not all that interested in my nachos, I work on them anyway while I wait for him to speak with me again.

"What about the second thing?" he asks at last. "You said it was less complicated."

"So you trust me with Rae?"

"I have to."

"That's encouraging."

"That's the situation."

"That you created."

"The second thing," he reminds me.

"I need to visit Phil."

He appears to question my definition of less complicated.

"I'll pretend to be Devin if you prefer," I offer.

"Your performance would be up to date, since you've clearly been talking to him."

"He found me at the Pep Rivers Desert Resort and Ponzi scheme."

"And he told you something about Phil," Marlowe gathers.

"He's going stardust before his parents get here."

"He wouldn't be the first. It's not uncommon."

"Phil's parents are great people who really love him. They nurtured him. They were devastated when he died. They started a tutoring program in his name."

"Then why won't he wait for them?"

"He's developed a theory about what happens next."

"After what?"

"After stardust."

"Nothing happens after stardust."

"You're sure?"

"As far as we know."

"It's been well-established, by you, that you don't know much. To paraphrase your own words, you're a cog in a wheel."

"Still," he grins away my reminder. "I think we would have heard something by now."

"But would you remember it?"

"Something that big?" he grows defensive. "I think we'd manage to keep it in mind."

"But if you heard it thousands of years ago..."

"That kind of thing wouldn't come up just once."

"If it came up by mistake," I propose. "If someone higher up let it slip, they would make sure it never happened again."

"What exactly is the Phil theory?" he returns to the roots of our conversation. "What does he think happens post-stardust?"

"Let me visit him, and you can listen in."

He chews on the offer.

"That could be interesting," he concedes.

"It will definitely be interesting. Shall I pretend to be Devin?"

"What about the second part of the second thing? Part two of your visit with Phil?"

"Definitely not the easiest thing to ask," I hedge. "Probably the hardest, in fact. On this visit. Not the hardest thing to ask anyone, ever. I guess the numerical order kind of worked after all. We could quibble over how to rank the previous requests, but this one is easily the hardest. Probably less complicated, oddly enough, but—"

"I'm waiting."

He is indeed waiting, in the way someone waits in a traffic jam, at a red light, or for the microwave oven to count down to zero and stop the leftovers from spinning.

My nachos look a lot more appealing, if not appetizing. I tear one off and could not say how it tastes. I treat it like people who chew gum use that to help them concentrate.

"If I can't convince Phil to stick around for his parents' sake," I say upon swallowing the distraction. "I'd like to arrange a call for them on the ghost portal so they can say good bye."

"You know the policy with the portal."

"When you listen to me and Phil talk, learn about his theory, hear how much he respects his parents, and how his love for them enters into his decision, maybe you'll reconsider."

"I doubt that."

"Let's see," I challenge him. "Let's go now."

"You're not done with your nachos," he nods toward my plate.

I search him for signs of a joke.

Finding none, I reach for a chip.

"Ha!" he breaks.

Our chairs disappear from underneath us and we fall to the floor, which is now the ground.

The ground is covered with cold, wet grass.

The sky is fresh off a rain, looking like a deep blue sea, the sun splashing and receding behind waves of clouds rolling across its surface. When the sun shines, the dewy meadow glistens. When the clouds take their turn, the low rocky hills appear to glow from within.

Smoke from a campfire rises from a rock that forms a ledge below the crest.

"Do I see a cave?" Marlowe wonders.

"You couldn't get us closer?" I ask.

"I didn't want him to see me."

"You can eavesdrop without being visible. I've seen you do it."

"You've seen me be invisible," he says out loud so I can hear how absurd it sounds.

"You know what I mean."

"I wanted to prove to you I made the trip."

"Thanks."

I take a deep breath. The recent storm has left its mark on the air.

"This is a lovely simulation," I caption the scent.

"A bit rugged," he scans the barren steppe. "But refreshing."

"Great place for a steak house."

He pretends to like the idea for a second.

"Shall we?" I gesture toward the smoke on the horizon.

"Go ahead," he gestures toward me. "I'll be there."

"You're not even walking half way?"

"I've proven my presence."

I glare back at him for the first couple of steps on my hike before facing the rock in the distance that hosts Phil and his fire.

Chapter Eight

There is a cave. Marlowe was right.

He may have known it rather than seen it.

The walk up the hill leaves me more out of breath than I have ever felt in the afterlife, and sweaty, which I have never been in the afterlife. To add to the anomalies, my pants are still damp in the rear from the grass, and my shoes are soaked.

Phil sits in front of the cave, manning his small fire, dressed in the tatters of what was once casual Friday attire.

I nearly ask why his simulation is so inconvenient and uncomfortable, but look for something nice to say instead.

The sight of the valley from above catches my eye as I catch my breath. The wet grass takes what it can from the dapples of sunlight and runs the shine across its blades.

"Nice view," I say, which is true.

"I didn't invite you," he keeps his eyes on the fire.

"I got a pass."

Phil shakes his head.

"Even in heaven it's who you know."

He reaches for a handful of sticks and tosses it on the fire. They crackle and hiss upon landing.

"I thought the next step was a world full of people who work together."

"It is," he stays focused on the flame.

"Then why the isolation?"

"The Next Earth will be natural, not invented. The more things we made up, the farther apart we got. Everyone behind their walls and in their bubbles. The afterlife is the ultimate expression of that tragedy."

"You've thought a lot more about this since we last spoke."

"I'm not sure how far back Next Earth takes us, but if it goes way back, I want to be prepared. I want to pull my weight. The rugged individual is a product of modern conveniences. In the real world, the world we were once part of before we starting making things up, being an individual was a death sentence. We had to be in a community if we wanted to live."

"I think you might be on to something."

He finally looks at me, checking for sincerity.

I seem to pass the inspection, but need to press on.

"They probably load you up on arrival with all the survival skills you need."

"No," he insists. "They don't. That would be fake. The skills have to be real."

"How does avoiding your parents prove those skills?"

"Sacrifice!" he stands. "How often do I have to explain this?"

"One more time," I handle the request with care.

"Everything is granted here."

Posturing aside, he clearly appreciates the opportunity to run through his philosophy again.

"Every wish, every desire," he starts to pace. "You cannot indulge that and expect to pass the test. Even if you limit your requests, there is no give, only take. No chance to show you understand the risks and rewards of any decision of any consequence."

"You're using your parents to prove yourself."

"What else is there?" he comes to a stop. "Who else is there? Who's coming into this place that holds any meaning for me?"

"You already have people here who think you're wonderful."

"That's nice," he softens. "Thank you. I appreciate it. But as much as I've enjoyed getting to know you, and some other people I didn't know all that well on earth, the stakes aren't high. And there's no way I can create them here. I can't invent a wife, invent a family of projections. My parents are the only real bond I have. They're the only sacrifice I have to offer."

"Without their permission."

"That's how sacrifice works, Devin. That's how love works. Heartbreak and pain don't ask for permission. They just happen."

"Maybe Next Earth is just the good stuff."

"How would we know it's good?" he quizzes me.

"Because we've experienced it before," I guess.

"And we know it can all go away at any moment," he reaches the peak of his argument.

Marlowe cuts in.

"Just like that," he adds a flourish to the end of Phil's sentence.

He stands on the edge of the ledge facing us, first looking at Phil while extending his explanation of what drives the good, then at me.

"I hope this means you like what you're hearing," I say.

"Is this your connection?" Phil asks me. "The guy who got you in here?"

"I'm not a guy," Marlowe approaches the fire. "But then neither is he."

They both look at me.

My shock at being outed is overwhelmed by the excitement of what it means.

"We're on?" I ask Marlowe.

"This guy gets it," he points at Phil. "I've always wanted to say that." I smile at Phil.

Phil still wants an answer to his first question.

"Am I really the only guy here?" he expands on it.

"Yes," Marlowe maintains the lead. "I'm on the regional board of this section of this era of the afterlife. So, no, I'm not human, but I've taken a human form for so long I'm not sure what I am."

He holds for laughter that neither of us provide.

Upon waiting for a lengthy few seconds, he proceeds with the introductions.

"And this is Devin Orr's clone," he nods in my direction.

"Clone?" Phil asks him at first, then looks at me.

"When we last hung out we were riding jet skis with dolphins," I say. "It's been the real Devin ever since."

He runs through his memories of before and after.

"That explains a lot," he concludes.

"Which I assume means original Devin doesn't compare to the new, improved version," I fish for an answer with a joke for bait.

Phil needs more space before he can embrace any humor in the situation.

"He ordered me to make his life easier," I offer more information while waiting for a bite. "Then lost his life in a scuba diving accident."

"How did you get here before him?" he wonders. "Did he get rid of you before he died?"

"I can go back and forth," I roll out the thumbnail version of my bio developed over the course of my travels. "When I'm put in storage on earth, in a deep sleep, here I am."

His eyes provide a glimpse of the old Phil, the sense of wonder he wore so peacefully when he used to make new friends in the afterlife, rather than indulge the same old earthbound fantasies carried out by apparently every other resident. That alone would seem to guarantee a passing grade on the test he has convinced himself he needs to take.

"We've been working together," Marlowe wants back in.

"Doing what?" Phil asks.

"Helping people on earth get to a good place before they get to our place."

"That sounds tricky."

"It can be," Marlowe walks around the fire closer to Phil. "Communication in particular can pose a challenge. But we found a way to keep in touch while he's on earth."

As thrilled as I am to discover the Dedmons are allowed to use the portal, Marlowe still has to extend the invitation and Phil has to accept it. Marlowe explains where ghosts come from, how he and his colleagues explored the use of those rips between the worlds to talk to people, and the standing date we arranged around the portal created by the ghost of Richard Cloud Rabbit and his hatred of air conditioning.

Phil does not seem terribly surprised by it all, a posture I suppose becomes more possible the longer someone exists in the afterlife, and the fantastic becomes the norm.

"When you said I get it," he asks Marlowe. "Does that mean I'm right about what happens after stardust?"

"No," Marlowe sustains his honesty. "Maybe. Probably not. None of us know. I just like your attitude."

Phil moves closer to him and appears to accept the offer to speak with his parents.

I could hear what they say to each other if I listened closely, but find myself immersed in the visual of them conversing behind a veil of smoke and fire. Two such important forces in my life, and I wonder what to call them. Phil is no longer a person. Marlowe never was. They are something, saying something about something to one another. I probably know what it is, but not the details.

Phil walks out from behind the smoky screen and takes a turn next to me. We stare at the fire for a while.

I deliver news from earth that may also be one last plea to wait for his folks, if he is at all persuadable at this point.

"Your parents started a foundation in your name that provides tutors for kids whose families can't afford one."

"That sounds like them. Did you help?"

"With the funding. I said they could do whatever they want, and that's what they did."

He looks into the fire as though he can see through it to the families helped by the foundation with his name on it.

"You really are better company than the original," he says.

"Thank you."

"I'm not just saying that to make up for how stand-offish I was earlier."

"Would you mind if I tell Devin the next time I see him?"

"You probably shouldn't."

"I'll try not to. But I'm sure I'll end up blurting it out when we bicker again."

"You do that a lot?"

"Not that I've ever had a sibling, or been a human being for that matter, but I get the impression that with the two of us, it's like having a very competitive relationship with a twin brother, only without the love."

Phil appreciates the analogy with a laugh that is more felt than heard. He gives me a hug, as though trying to make up for what I lack with my mock twin. When he releases me, he returns to his original spot by the fire and sits back down, legs crossed, his back to the cave, looking through the flames at the valley below.

Marlowe and I make eye contact and he leads the way.

We walk along the ridge, rather than back down the hill.

"Not an easy path," he notes as we jump from rock to rock. "But dry, and we can catch more of the view before moving on."

"Thank you for letting me use the phone."

"Forgive us for being so impatient," he tells me over his shoulder. "We should have understood that getting good at this job would take longer than we imagined, and more visits than we anticipated."

"I'm not sure I'll ever be truly good," I scan the rocks for the next best landing spot. "But I'll keep trying as long as Trisha keeps sending me."

"Since you don't have to do anything for her on this trip, you should indulge in a fun or relaxing simulation while you wait for the pull. Visit that seaside town Phil designed where you parked the jet skis. Raise a glass to him, treat yourself."

"There's actually one more errand I'd like to run before I do that kind of thing."

"Oh?" he holds his ground on his latest stone.

"I want to visit Elijah," I stop on a rock of my own.

"Again?" Marlowe turns to face me.

"Talking to Phil got me thinking about him. Eli feels things so deeply, I could see him developing a New Earth philosophy of his own. I want to make sure he's still planning on sticking around until June gets here."

"All right," he grins.

"What?" I address his expression.

"He's not in the club."

"That's fine. I'll meet him wherever he is. I'm not adopting a projection, so it doesn't matter how many of them are around. I'm going with the customer service rep routine. I figure I might as well, since I'm there to gauge his satisfaction."

His grin holds.

"I don't think Eli is the kind of person who experiences satisfaction," he says.

I see what he means. I consider a different approach, or a different vocabulary.

"I'll gauge his yearning to make amends with his mother, maybe his friends."

"Not his father," he reminds me.

"You may not have been a fan of my visit to Pep's paradise but—"

"I was definitely not a fan."

"But now I know why Eli longs to keep his distance."

"Longing and yearning," Marlowe muses. "That's our Eli."

"Satisfaction in longing and yearning," I build on his meditation.

"That could be his campaign slogan."

"Campaign?"

"You'll see," he turns and hops onto the next best rock.

I turn toward the valley view before using our thoughts on Eli to enter his bubble.

"Don't forget," Marlowe calls back to me from atop his latest boulder. "Do something decadent after you check in with him."

The valley rises up toward the ridgeline, then the ridgeline lowers down to the valley. They take turns. Valley up, ridgeline down, back and forth. When valley and hilltop meet at last, a thin river of twists and turns starts running through it, a stream so skinny that most of the grassy floor fans out from each bank rather than wind up underwater. The clouds evaporate, surrendering all sky to the sun. The grass dries, going from green and damp to yellow and brittle, while the dusty ground beneath the blades grows more visible. Scrub oak and cottonwood trees spring in squiggly lines along the shore, and in bushy clusters farther away from the sandy riverbed. Within those knots of shrubs and trees, an occasional tent materializes, or a lean-to made of large empty boxes, or a tarp hung between branches.

When the simulation settles, I am standing alongside one of the encampments, wondering which shelter may have Eli inside of it, much like when I found myself in the manicured world of Grandpa Vale. Rather than a gunshot, however, my first clue as to where my target may be comes from the sound of his voice. I recognize his tone too late to make out what he says, but it carries the calm charm I recall from the club and continue to hear about from those who knew him.

An older woman emerges from a tent three shrubs away and zips the door behind her. She might be elderly, or she might be middle-aged and whittled away from exposure. She is draped in layers, like Trisha, but layers she has found, rather than bought, and to hide in, rather than make an impression. We nod at each other as she approaches.

"Is Eli in there?" I ask.

She adds an extra nod while passing by.

I walk to the tent and hunch toward the zipper.

"Elijah Rivers?" I inquire.

"That's me," his voice responds.

"I'm here on behalf of the Afterlife Outreach Department. We're surveying a random sample of our residents on their afterlife experience. I was hoping to get feedback from you and include it in our research."

"Sure," he says. "Come on in. The zipper's unlocked."

I unzip the door and duck into the tent. Like Phil, he has not scrubbed any discomfort from his simulation. The hot air has a whiff of body odor, not as pungent as I imagine the real version would be, but my sense of smell may be overwhelmed by the sight of how much older he looks.

"Hello," I cloak my surprise by sitting and fidgeting for a comfortable position.

"Hey there," he watches me squirm.

Even if exposure to the elements has contributed to his appearance, his base age is still far more advanced than when his band plays the club. I settle in and embrace the bombshell.

"I don't think I've ever seen a young resident go elderly."

"Just for this simulation," he says. "The homeless camp."

"So it really is a homeless camp."

"Do I look like a Boy Scout troop leader?"

"More like a hunting guide."

"How about a mayor?" he asks.

"You mean a nickname? Like when a colorful local is called the Mayor of Echo Park, or the Mayor of Beale Street? I can see that."

"I mean an actual mayor."

"Of the town outside this riverbed?"

"Of the riverbed."

I feel as though I am out of guesses. He explains.

"It may not look like it, but we have a system in place here. We help each other out, share food and necessities. And we elect leaders. When I was living on earth, I lived in this riverbed for a while, but downstream, where there are no rules, where it's every person for themselves. I wasn't even worthy of being in the nice part of a homeless camp."

"Redemption."

"That's right."

"Has it worked? Are you satisfied with your experience?"

"For the most part, yes."

The leftover part leaves me worried.

"Good to know," I play my part. "What do you find lacking?"

"Nothing that's your fault," he explains. "I was young, like you said. Young in terms of an afterlife. So I have a ways to wait until people I love get here."

"What about your father?"

I half expect Marlowe to pop up in the tent and interrupt me.

I assumed Eli would be agitated. He does look confused for a moment as to how I know about his father, then recalls the job title I announced outside his tent, and faces the question of his father with composure.

"Maybe I'll see him after some of the others arrive," he says. "He just can't be the first one I face."

"Were things that bad?"

"I frightened people when I was around, made them anxious. Then I would disappear and make them feel helpless and sad. But not Dad."

"You don't think he cares?"

"I don't think it's personal. I don't think he cares about much in general. He likes to play. Nothing seems to bother him. And that bothers someone like me."

"Someone who cares too much?"

"You know the type," he smiles.

"The type who makes a great mayor."

"This place was my chance," he gestures as if we are outside the tent surveying the shallow waters and makeshift sanctuaries. "I stumbled upon chances now and then when I would wander, but this one was the best. It was an entryway back into the world, an apprenticeship. If I could work my way upstream from the chaos downstream, I could make my way back to reality. Baby steps."

His movements have stopped. Anything he sees is inside of himself.

"I didn't want to disappoint anyone anymore," he says. "That's what happened whenever I went back. They would get frustrated and blame themselves. So I stopped going back."

"Now you're the one waiting for them."

"I am," he eases into the exterior once more.

"You're not going stardust before they get here?"

He answers by glaring at me.

"No," he says anyway.

"Just asking," I apologize. "It's part of the job."

"I finally have some peace of mind," he catches himself betraying that peace. "I need to use it to face everyone and thank them for trying. Especially Mom."

I generate an exit line to thank him for his responses, but before I can use it, a young woman pokes her head in. She looks as though she went to an outdoor music festival and never left.

"Oh," she was not expecting to see anyone other than Eli. "Sorry. It was unzipped."

"That's okay, Luna," Eli assures her. "What do you need?"

"The septic tank has a crack in it."

"Dang," Eli ponders their options. "Any leads on a replacement?"

Luna appears doubtful.

"Do we still have epoxy in the bag?" he moves on to plan B.

"We do."

"Let's just fix it for now while we keep our ear to the ground. I'll be out after we're done in here."

"You could replace it," I remind them.

I snap my fingers to illustrate how easy it could be.

They look at each other.

"He's from Public Relations," Eli informs her.

"Ah," she glows with recognition. "The Man."

They enjoy their callback to the old anti-establishment cliché.

"I love being called a man," I join in on the enjoyment. "Even cynically."

"Interesting," Eli says. "I would think you'd be tired of people after working with them for thousands of years."

"I got tired of them by the time I was twelve," Luna says.

"I'm sorry to hear that," I say.

"Want to tell him what happened?" Eli prompts Luna.

"If you don't mind sitting through the same old story again."

"I'll stand this time," he gets up. "Shall we head outside?"

I agree and we join Luna in front of the tent.

"My mother had a string of horrible boyfriends when I was a kid," she looks toward the river rather than at us, as if her audience is sitting on its banks, and we are watching from backstage. "I would think the last one was the worst, then she would somehow find an even bigger loser. The earliest ones were just lazy idiots. They'd stare at me a little too long every so often, but no violence. Until the list started getting longer and we were reaching the bottom. The last one before I ran away was by far the worst. Gold medal, major league worthless, and he knew it, and took it out on us. By then Mom was relying so heavily on the boyfriend carousel we didn't have a place of our own. We would live with her latest mistake. When we left one moron, she had the next moron lined up. I figured this was no different. So when she corralled me out bed while the monster was asleep, and we drove away, like we had a bunch of times before, I was happy. Usually I would be annoyed. But this guy was so beyond awful, I was all smiles. I was actually kind of proud of Mom, since that was the nicest house we had ever lived in. I thought she was going to stick with him for the big screen TV and the recliner couch. When we parked in the rear lot of the twenty-four hour diner, I thought we were going to celebrate, split a sundae or some Belgian waffles."

She seems to forget we are next to her. There is the river and herself, and nothing else.

"But we didn't get out of the car. Mom turned off the engine, put her seat all the way back, and curled up into the fetal position on her side so she didn't have to face me. What did I need her for at that point? Why should I stay? Okay, she left the worst man in the world. Way to go, Mom. But she couldn't see this coming? She didn't have a plan? She just suddenly realized he was the worst man in the world? I felt like a dog who belonged to a homeless person. We were on a never-ending walk. I had no regrets about leaving her. The hardest part was trying to close the car door without making any noise. I was on the streets for a couple of days before I found my way to the riverbed. The mayor at the time and the council took me in. After I settled down and felt human again, they got me help. I lucked out in the foster care system, wound up with decent parents. I was only here for a couple of days, but it was an important couple of days, and I never forgot them. So when Eli started this simulation and sent out a group invite, I was excited."

She faces us.

"Can you believe that?" she says with pride rather than dismay. "Excited to spend part of my afterlife in a homeless camp."

"It makes the fun simulations all the more fun," Eli cracks, hoping to let in more lightness.

"I know I came here to speak with Eli," I take a chance. "But I'm curious. Did you have any contact with your mother after that?"

"Don't you know?" Eli runs interference.

"If I ask around," I play the part. "But no, not off the top of my head. Our department is far down the ranks when it comes to being all-knowing."

"Not on earth," Luna cuts to her answer. "And she went stardust before I got here."

"She didn't do the work," Eli says to me before I bother to make any allusions. "We have a proverb in the riverbed: 'Simulations don't solve problems.' They don't tell you that in orientation."

"Would you like to suggest a revision?" I ask.

"Will it make a difference?"

"Maybe. If there appears to be a critical mass of the same suggestion."

"So you have a petition process."

"Uh..."

"This place," Eli shakes his head. "Infinite sex, travel, and entertainment. But God forbid you should want to get something done."

"I'll look into it."

"That's very reassuring," he deadpans.

"He's just doing his job," Luna offers a tepid defense.

"Tell him the rest of your story," he says to her. "It might come in handy. One of those bureaucratic bodies must have a heart in it somewhere."

She looks apologetic, either because she feels she has interrupted my task too much already, or because she pities my character and the role he plays in the great machine.

"I was disappointed Mom was already gone," Luna proceeds. "I wanted to reach out. I felt guilty later on in life when I was contacted about her death. She was living out of another car. I don't know where she got it. Probably from yet another loser. I was going to sell it sight unseen, make a few bucks, but was curious. I decided to drive it myself to a used car lot. First I emptied out all the crap inside, which didn't feel like anything, just a chore. But sitting in the empty car afterwards was different. There were a few little things left over. Cigarette butts in the ashtray, a couple of paper coffee cups on the passenger seat floor. Stuff with her DNA on it, if anyone wanted to bother investigating her death. I found myself imaging her behind the wheel, where I was sitting, talking to herself, bursting into tears all of a sudden, then yelling at anyone who made the slightest wrong move on the road. She loved it when that happened. It was a chance to feel superior. She'd let them have it, scream out the window, then talk about it for way too long after the fact. I thought of all the time she spent sitting there, staring out the windows. I felt whatever haunted her was haunting me. The empty space was occupying me rather than the other way around. The space left room for stories, and the stories became more moving than the person who lived in it. I thought about that empty space long after I left the car on the lot and looked forward to meeting her again. But that never happened. I finally got here and lost her again."

She concludes with a smile.

"I'm older than I look," she says.

"You and everyone else," I comment.

"Almost everyone," Eli proudly refers to himself.

"The home office wanted to survey typical residents," I feed his self-flattery. "I insisted we could learn more from those with an unconventional approach to paradise."

"You mean weirdos?" Luna quips.

"He doesn't want to confuse us with technical jargon," Eli absorbs her jab.

"I'll let you wrap it up," she eases her way out.

"See you down at the septic tank," Eli says.

"I'll bring the epoxy."

"Sounds like a party," I say.

"Nice meeting you," she tells me.

"Likewise."

We watch her walk away.

"She seems real," I remark.

"She usually is. Sometimes a projection fills in if we've called a meeting and she can't get away from another simulation. It's a good pro, as far as projections go. Knows our rhythms."

"Tells her story well."

"I'm pretty sure that was really her."

Luna veers down a path through a thicket of shrubs and trees. I keep looking in the direction where she used to be.

"Her backstory reminds me of someone," I say. "Someone I hope winds up with a happy ending of her own."

"Doesn't everyone have a happy ending here? Technically speaking?"

"Fulfilling might be a better word."

"It usually is."

I turn to face Eli.

"Thank you, Mr. Rivers," I extend my hand.

"That's it?"

"I don't need to ask a lot of questions. Being around you for a few minutes is more enlightening than an hour-long interview with most residents."

"Even if that's not true, it sounds so nice. I'll take it."

He shakes my hand.

"Delighted to hear you'll be staying a while," I say.

"Don't be a stranger," he says.

I release my grip and think to myself that I have no choice. I was meant to be a stranger. I would say I was born to be one, but I was not born.

Chapter Nine

I try everything I can come up with to clear my head. Quiet contemplation does not work. I walk around the Laguna Beach-Monterey combo town Phil generated while on a jet ski. I sit on the patios of its cafes and bars along its cliffs and beaches, thinking of ways to approach Rae about how mulligans work. My other contacts who are due for revelations inspire some tension of their own, but her case is the most challenging.

Transparency is my only option with the Dedmons. No head fakes apply when using a ghost portal to take a call from your dead son.

The dreamscape angle I have with June is ours alone. If and when I use it on someone else, it becomes a con, rather than a bond. And I want to feel a bond with both June and Rae.

So I take the words of Marlowe to heart and dive into a series of indulgent simulations to take my mind off of the task ahead and hope the answer will sneak up on me while I am busy flying over a super bloom of wildflowers in a hot air balloon, skiing down a mountain covered in frozen margarita snow, and navigating through a massive school of hammerhead sharks in a personal submarine. But I cannot shake the nagging wonder of how on earth I can tell Rae that her son Rory is a girl, an abandoned toddler named Brittania, who is couch surfing her way around the Bullhead City, Laughlin, and Needles Tri-State area under the care of her broke grandma.

An idea finally splashes cold water on my confusion while I park the submarine in the hull of a luxury yacht full of women wearing nothing but flimsy hospital gowns waving at me from the main deck. Maybe the shame of giving in to temptation shakes the answer out of me, or realizing all the women I fabricated look a lot like Gina, leader of the conspiracy to murder Devin and use me to steal his money, but as I attach the sub to a winch, it dawns on me that while I may not have a clear sense of how to inform Rae, I know someone who might.

I never thought I would visit Tip again, or at least not for a while.

The list of marks he provided is long enough to last Trisha well beyond what her thirst for revenge on the valley allows, especially considering the several members beyond the top three. By her own admission, she is starting to leave herself open to a level of scrutiny she may not be able to manage, and needs to pace herself and lower her profile. Plus Tip was so crabby when we met, I was not interested in a relationship that was anything other than transactional, and neither was he.

When I climb the stairs and reach the main deck, it is no longer filled with Gina lookalikes.

It is also no longer made of wood, on a boat, moored to an anchor in an open sea.

Instead it is made of brick, on shore, in a forest overlooking a lake.

Piano music seeps in from behind the French doors of the same supper club where I last left Tip. Laughter competes with the music, a slight twist from my last visit, when everyone listened in silence to the piano player. The laughter becomes a bigger twist when I enter and discover Tip is the source.

He sits at the piano bar with a woman I assume is his wife, since he looks the same age as my last visit, his earth exit age, and she appears to have embraced the same stance, as though they want to pick up where they left off, rather than reimagine the past. The consistency of his appearance cannot hide the fact he is a changed man. It may even enhance the change. If I had not caught him in the act of laughing, his face would betray him. I watch them together and whether he is listening to her or talking, he always seems to be on the verge of laughter, or recovering from a recent bout. I would be reluctant to interrupt them, they are so in love, but it is clearly the kind of love earned over decades. Any time spent together is relished, but not at the expense of the world around them, in which they are eager participants.

For when Tip sees me, he brightens and beckons, and his wife trusts that anyone he calls over is worth meeting.

He turns in his chair to greet me as I take my place a step back from the space between them.

"Did you burn through the list already?" he teases with a light pat on my arm.

"One load of dirty laundry at a time," I recite my rule.

"Missy," he introduces me. "This is the guy I was telling you about. The one who can bounce between life and afterlife."

"Ah," she adds me up. "Devin Orr's clone."

"Missy!" Tip performs a rebuke. "Sorry, Dev."

I have no recollection of being called Dev, in either my memory bank or Devin's, but I like it.

"We're all clones here," she defends herself. "Aren't we?"

"Not exactly human," Tip sees her point.

"Something way beyond," she pulls him in for a kiss.

"Something higher," he accepts her affection.

"But I had a head start," I claim at the conclusion of their kiss. "What with not being born human."

They laugh in acknowledgment of how obnoxious they can be.

"Which reminds me," Tip says as his chuckle runs out. "I appreciate what you said about Jesus."

"Remind me what I said about Jesus," I honestly cannot recall.

"How busy he must be, how many requests he must get."

"That was you?" Missy exclaims. "It's been very comforting. Thank you."

"In fact," Tip reveals. "We withdrew our request."

"Really?"

"Jesus should be able to enjoy himself," he nods.

"He had such a hard life on earth," Missy further builds their logic.

"Nobody's earned paradise more than Christ," Tip keeps the rationale humming.

"With so many people here who love him," Missy makes eyes at Tip. "He has the best version of paradise there is."

"Amen," Tip joins her in a gazing contest. "And I speak from experience. Once you got here, Love Cub, the afterlife turned into paradise."

"To he who has much," I hop on board their train of thought. "More will be given."

"Hey," Tip spins with glee in my direction. "I didn't think you had faith. You or Devin."

"Certain passages ring true."

"So what brings you here?" Tip keeps facing me with a hand on Missy's knee. "I should have asked earlier, but I've been distracted lately."

He gives her knee a squeeze.

"Perhaps we could talk in private," I suggest.

"Anything you say stays right here," he says. "Because where else would it go?"

He laughs and Missy joins him.

"Okay," I cannot deny his point. "It's about one of my earth redemption projects."

"Ah yes," he recollects. "The good stuff."

"I have a woman who lost a child young enough to earn a mulligan."

"A mulligan?" Missy is unfamiliar with the term.

"You didn't learn about those in orientation?" Tip asks her.

"You have to ask," I say. "They like to keep things moving."

"I was eager to see you," she tells Tip. "My only question was how soon I could."

He is flattered.

With no end in sight for their honeymoon phase, I take it upon myself to catch her up.

"It's a do-over for someone so young or otherwise lacking in experience to create much of an afterlife."

"I see," she says, still more interested in her husband than proof of reincarnation.

"Anyway," I go back to informing Tip. "I thought it might be comforting for the mother to know the spirit of her child lives on, and my contacts here were able to supply me with the baby's new identity."

"Oh my," Missy senses trouble.

"You want to tell her," Tip hopes he is wrong.

"You don't think it's a good idea?" I address their reactions.

"An intriguing one," Tip grants. "But good? Eh..."

"No," Missy is more blunt. "She can find out when she gets here."

"But there won't be a reunion," I say.

"Why not?" Missy asks.

"It's up to the child who's been reborn," I explain. "But they pretty much never know they're a mulligan, because they have to ask, and they pretty much never do."

"How convenient," she sniffs.

"They've lived a whole new life as an adult," Tip considers the administrative standpoint. "Maybe the play is to discourage the mother from asking when she gets here."

"Not a chance," she glares at both of us. "Take it from a fellow member of the motherhood."

"So why not let her know while she's still on earth?" I ask.

"Do you really need me to explain it?"

"I know it's a lot for her to take in," I acknowledge. "But the new kid is stuck in a life of poverty and unlikely to cycle out of it, and my client has the means to help."

"Have her donate to charity," Missy maintains.

"That little soul could have wound up anywhere," I appeal to their faith. "But was reborn within a one-day drive from the original mother."

"Have her donate to a church," Missy adjusts her vocabulary in kind.

"Where exactly is the new child?" Tip asks.

"Needles," I answer.

He turns to Missy.

"We really need to do something," he insists.

"You're kidding," Missy chides him.

"Remember my cousin Carlos?"

"He lived in Laughlin."

"It's right across the state line."

"They spend time there, too," I chime in. "The toddler and her grandma couch surf and live out of their car."

"So let's drag the grieving mother into it," Missy grabs her drink and takes a long sip.

"You're so good with people," I forge ahead with my pitch to Tip. "You know how to reach them, no matter how challenging the situation may be. I've come up with a few ways to drop some knowledge on earth while keeping my secret, but this is way beyond the great beyond. This is a next-level balancing act."

"What about the people you work with on this side?" he asks.

"They're not people," I lament. "They don't know how the world works."

"Sounds to me like they know exactly how the world works," Missy cuts in. "Only a lifelong bureaucrat or a very gifted, diabolical consultant could come up that red tape road block for the parents of mulligans."

"They may have a knack for bureaucracy," I pose. "But when it comes to healthy human interactions, all they have to go on are the fantasies of residents trying to reshape the world they left to their liking."

Tip thinks, or it turns out may have just been in preparation for the pleading look he gives Missy.

"Fine," she relents and hunches back over the piano bar to focus on the music. "Blow your cover. And her mind. To bits."

"She has a point," Tip pivots off it toward me. "Revealing too much puts you both at risk."

"That's where you come in," I take aim. "How do I withhold while I inform?"

He takes a cleansing breath.

"You say she has means," he explores a notion. "What kind of tax bracket are we talking about?"

"They live in your old zip code, but bought a foreclosure."

"Power," he says, now zeroed in on the task at hand, as if back on earth enmeshed in a strategy session. "That's our angle. Your angle."

"Power," I ponder the word as his cue to continue.

"Access to it," he follows through. "She understands how it works, given where she lives, but probably falls on a lower level than someone like Devin."

"Money can't buy access to the afterlife," I provide another prompt.

"It buys access to people who have those kinds of connections."

"Mystics?" I scoff. "Fortune tellers? I don't care how high-priced they are, a fraud is a fraud."

"Don't be that specific. Great power is mysterious to most. Its highest levels inspire paranoia and tales of conspiracy. Embrace the mystery, Dev. Stay vague."

I process his advice while Missy groans as the piano player launches into "The Windmills of Your Mind".

"By request?" I ask Tip with a nod toward the performance.

"A bit too on-the-nose," Missy grouses.

He ignores us both and further explains his proposition.

"Groundbreaking tech first benefits the privileged," he submits. "If it ever reaches the underprivileged at all. Communicating with the dead and the reincarnated wouldn't be any different, would it? Or should I say, isn't it?"

We exchange a look, both of us on the verge of a grin, but Missy interrupts us before we get there, leaving us instead with smirks.

"Let's have a toast," she suggests. "Can we buy you a drink?"

"I should go before Trisha pulls me back," I excuse myself. "The pull can get messy, and I don't want to disrupt this lovely setting."

"Heaven forbid," she jabs.

Tip rubs her back while he sends me off with a story.

"I finally went to a Pep Rivers party."

"You did?"

"He said he was very happy you convinced me to go."

A short laugh barks out of me.

"Tip played along," Missy adds.

"That sim might come in handy," he explains. "If you ever make it through our list, there's a bottomless pit of con artists in that desert. Just replace the Tip list with a Pep party."

"And you're a bottomless pit of sage advice," I shake his hand and apologize to Missy for the intrusion before exiting through the French doors in time to see the water in the lake start to slosh slowly back and forth, as though in a bucket in the back of a truck being driven on a winding road.

I sprint to the edge of the patio and leap, spread eagle, as if aiming for a perfect ten in a belly flop contest.

After five seconds of falling, instead of hitting the surface of the water, I pass through the usual dark void, somersault onto my back, and wind up prone in the examination room of Trisha's office complex.

I give her the name of the Moldovan art dealer and leave without saying good bye.

On the road to visit Rae, I run through different ways I can explain how mulligans work.

I decide to start by discussing updates from Everything concerning her foundation. I have not contacted him since my return, so I can rely on her to let me know where the process stands, and react to the current status with sincerity. Wading into the weeds of logistics keeps me in the moment and calms my nerves.

When I transition to the primary purpose of my visit, I preface the move by saying I understand what I am about to tell her sounds insane, but since I sold my company and ventured into a variety of different fields controlled by powerful people, I have learned there is much more to the world than most of us can see. In some cases we are not allowed to, in others we are not able to, but thanks to an injection of great wealth into my life, I have been invited to enough demonstrations of the miraculous to remove any doubts that anything is possible. One of those things is reincarnation.

As soon as I say that word, she will likely suspect where I am going with what I am saying. I focus at first on Brittania, and stay away from Rory, in order to ease into the connection. I tell the sad, infuriating story of her mother, and the sad, heartening story of her grandmother. I explain the good fortune of having them so close, driving distance, even if it does involve some state line roulette.

But the story of Britt has to wait, because as soon as I mention reincarnation, Rae rewrites my script.

"You know the Letter Writer," she hopes.

"Oh," I feel foolish for not anticipating this. "You follow that story."

"I'm a proud member of Team Receivers."

I reach for a sip of the iced tea she poured from a pitcher she brought out to the patio where we sit in her backyard. I scold myself for the oversight as I tilt the glass, swallow my frustration along with the tea, then compose a response as I exhale and return the glass to the tabletop. With a slow pan around her garden to appreciate its beauty and ground me in the present, like I was minutes ago when discussing foundation paperwork, I roll out the new approach.

"No," I say. "I don't know the Letter Writer. But I know people who do. I know someone who knows someone who knows him."

"And they told you that he told them that reincarnation is real."

"I wasn't going to divulge my source," I take the path she has carved. "In case you were more of a Team Deceivers type, or oblivious to the whole thing."

This direction has a lot of promise. Never mind me. How could Tip fail to see it?

"I wasn't that into it until Rory died," she says. "Then I started to hang on every post, wanting to believe, hoping it was proof that I was going to see him later on, in the next life."

I sit and watch her have a realization of her own.

"Reincarnation," she repeats the word that led us here.

I let her stare at me as she struggles to decide whether she is receiving good or bad news.

"Am I not going to see him when I get there?" she asks.

"The very young get another chance."

"I guess that's only fair," she manages to say before breaking down.

She puts her head in her hands and doubles over, howling in pain, as if kicked in the midsection.

I look away, trying to give her a sliver of privacy without leaving her. I see a cluster of lilies volunteering in a damp corner of the yard, and search for more of them until the howling stops.

She remains bent over in her chair, breathing heavily. When her heart rate slows, and the timing seems right, I share the saga of Brittania and her grandmother, like I had planned to earlier. Rae keeps her head down for the whole story.

"That's who Rory is now?" she asks when I finish.

She uproots her gaze from the ground to glare at me.

I nod.

"What am I supposed to do with that information?"

I wordlessly let her know it is up to her.

"Maybe I'll switch to Team Deceivers," she says.

I smile.

She nearly does as well.

"I debated whether to tell you," I say. "I had my link to the Letter Writer for a while, but never bothered using it. Then when I met you, it occurred to me that young children were never the subject of any letters. I asked them about a case like Rory out of curiosity. I thought of it as a hypothetical question, but they came back with all that detail. I decided to go ahead and let you know because by the time everyone hits the afterlife, it's too late. The separate lives have been led."

"Thank you," she says, but I am not certain she means it.

"If you want help getting in touch with anyone on the California side of their loop, social workers or just people who know them, give me or Everything a call."

"I'll need time," she returns to looking away from me. "Probably a lot of it."

"Understandable," I rise to let her start the clock. "I hope I did the right thing."

"I'll let you know," she says.

"I'll let myself out."

As I approach the house, a pair of marble nymphs with bob haircuts stand guard on each side of the rear entrance. They are carved into mischievous poses, as though not taking their job seriously.

"By the way," I am inspired to reach for some lightness before leaving.

"Yes?" she remains seated with her back to me.

"Do you happen to know if the previous owners of your house bought any pieces from a Moldovan art dealer?"

"We had no interaction with them and no interest."

"Just a heads-up," I try harder to sell the buoyancy. "If they did, some investigators might be stopping by with some questions."

"And I will have no answers."

I sense a lighter tone from her, but I might be hearing what I want to hear.

Chapter Ten

The Dedmons and I stand together, facing the space between the ice maker and the vending machine that features six different flavors of Doritos.

"This spot offers the clearest audio," I explain while we wait.

I have been transparent with them for the most part. They know my true identity now, and what I am capable of, but I made the portal call sound like an exclusive event, a one-off for their benefit that involved pulling a lot of strings. Telling them all of the above all at once may not have been ideal. There were a few weeks before the first Monday of the month I could have used to lay the foundation of a more gradual reveal, but decided it was best not to let any bizarre revelations linger before offering proof. The drive from their house to the hotel is two hours, and they did not say a word the whole way.

"Which tracks perfectly," I riff on the audio clarity a little more to fill the silence. "If you think of a portal as an engine, it needs to stay cool, so the ice maker helps. Then there's the aesthetics. This machine with the Doritos is way better than the one over there with the off-brand sodas."

They seem scared of me since the big reveal. I would feel more guilty if this was not such an urgent call. When they greeted me at their door, I was impressed with how put together they are as individuals, and how together they are as a couple. The meekness that marked them in mourning their son has been replaced by conviction as the foundation named in his honor flourishes. I am doing what I can to show them there is nothing to fear. Not just with jokes, but assurances their son is fine, that being able to speak with him is proof of the stellar reputation he has built.

"They don't allow just anybody to use the phone," I hype their boy. "If it's possible for you to have any more room in your hearts for any more pride, and I know space is limited because you've always been so proud of him, well, this may breech the levee."

Mrs. Dedmon assembles a wan smile.

Mr. Dedmon reaches for her hand and clutches it, as if reminding her not to talk to strangers.

The call starts to materialize.

"Ah," I remark. "Good. See? I'm not insane."

They are too busy staring at the vapors swirling in front of the machines to give me any credit for following through on my lunatic claims.

"We have to wait for Richard to make his speech first," I explain.

They look even more scared now that the scary thing I told them about is turning out to be true.

"Remember?" I review what I said would happen. "Richard Cloud Rabbit. This is his portal. He died protesting the arrival of air conditioning to the valley."

The voice of Richard spills through the apparition floating before us.

"He's speaking his native tongue," I remind them.

I keep my voice involved to keep the Dedmons from running.

"I think he has a good point in any language," I talk them through their shock. "If artificial air is needed to live someplace, maybe that's a sign it shouldn't be lived in. Like Phoenix. Do people really live in Phoenix? Or do they live in an air-conditioned bio-dome located in Phoenix?"

They at last look at me, but in horror.

"Don't worry," I tell them. "I'm not interrupting Richard. It's not even him. Just a loop of the speech he was making when the afterlife intersected with his place on earth."

I would be miffed about them ignoring the humor of my commentary, but they are far too terrified to notice anything other than what is terrifying them. I am confident the call will fix that, so I roll with my strategy, useless as it may be.

"Come to think of it," I chatter away. "Richard's philosophy very much mirrors Phil's philosophy. You'll see."

The ballad of Richard Cloud Rabbit fades and the voice of Marlowe bounces through the haze into the alcove.

"You there, Doc?"

"You know how I feel about that name."

"Are Mr. and Mrs. Dedmon with you?"

"They are."

And they look seconds away from mutual cardiac arrest.

"Please hold the line for Phil Dedmon," Marlowe announces.

"Mom?" Phil asks. "Dad?"

His voice unfreezes them.

They sob and hug each other.

"They need a moment, Phil," I tell him. "It's a lot to take in. I tried to prepare them, but I'm not sure that's possible."

"Probably not," he agrees. "But I understand time is limited on this line."

"It is."

"How can you sound so rational?" Mr. Dedmon asks his son while consoling his wife.

"This is my world now, Dad. It's normal to me. Someday it will be to you, too."

Both of his parents take comfort in his assurance.

"That sounds nice," Mrs. Dedmon tells her son. "We miss you."

"I miss you, too," Phil says. "Which is why I wanted to call you."

Phil sounds like he is caught up in the moment after all, and needs another moment to regain his composure before continuing.

"The current Mr. Orr can fill in more details later on if you want him to. Right, Devin?"

"Of course."

"Because I need to keep things moving before we lose the connection, and the most important thing I need to say is I love you. I love you both dearly. You might not understand anything else about what I have decided to do, but please understand that I love you."

"We love you too, son," says his mother.

"Is something wrong, son?" asks his father, confusion tiptoeing into his tone, and the look he shares with his wife.

"There is nothing you could have done differently," Phil proceeds with what he sounds prepared to say. "You were the best parents a boy like me could have. I've never had a moment of regret or resentment here in the afterlife, not one second. And I hope you've felt the same way since I've been here."

"We do," his mother speaks on their behalf.

"Absolutely," his father concurs.

"Good," Phil forges ahead. "Good. Because I'm afraid I won't be here when you arrive."

They wonder in a shocked hush which of them should holler "What!?"

"I'm convinced this isn't the end," he seizes on their silence. "I know in my heart there is another world after this one I'm in, another life past what everyone assumes is heaven, where only the most upstanding people end up, the people who maintain their dignity even when it doesn't seem to matter to anyone else."

He catches himself preaching and stops short.

"Like I said," he slows down. "Mr. Orr can expand on my beliefs if you want him to. We've had many a debate over them."

I offer the Dedmons an exaggerated nod of agreement, but they still appear unready to react to much of anything.

"Honorable people understand sacrifice," Phil says. "They know the price of love is pain. You not only loved me, but you did right by me. Not everyone does both. The fact you did makes me all the more confident in my decision. I don't think I could do it if we left anything unsaid, if we had anything unfinished between us. But we don't. You did your job beautifully. Anything beyond what we lived would be excessive, maybe even risky."

"You really can't stay?" his Mom asks.

"You could leave right after," his Dad adds.

"Make a projection of me," he suggests. "I've been here a while so they have lots to go on. It'll be a good one. Very accurate."

"Projection?" his father asks whichever one of us is willing to explain.

"We didn't get that far," I address both sides of the portal. "Lots to cover."

"Of course," Phil acknowledges. "Uh oh."

He can apparently tell seconds before us that the line is fading.

The fog dissipates from the air and condenses onto the glass of the vending machine.

"Thank you for the foundation," he squeezes in a last word before the portal closes.

"You're welcome," his mother whispers, knowing she is too late to be heard.

She swipes her hand across the foggy glass, hoping she can see him on the other side.

"Do you think he meant the tutoring foundation?" she keeps looking through the path she cleared. "Or do you think he meant his childhood? That kind of foundation."

"I don't think there's a wrong answer to that question," I say.

She inspects the machine as though it drives the rift between the worlds, rather than simply being located in the space where it operates.

"He sounds so smart," she reflects.

"Too smart for his own good," Mr. Dedmon leans his back against the wall of the small room.

"He's grown quite a bit," I submit. "And that's rare in those parts. Most people shrink. They degenerate into something pathetic. I know you're disappointed in his decision, but at some point you're going to be proud of it. I assure you."

"When we have a better understanding of where he is, I suppose," says Mr. Dedmon.

"That will help, yes."

"Well," he stands up straight, takes the two steps needed to stand behind his wife, and puts his arms around her. "Let's hear it."

"All of it," she grabs his arms and wraps them tighter around herself, pressing all four of their hands onto her belly. "Tell us about his growth, and how most people conduct themselves."

"And projections," says Mr. Dedmon. "Tell us about projections."

He chuckles into her neck.

She flinches but does not resist. Reflex gives way to affection.

The drive home is not enough time to learn all they want to know, so they take me out to dinner at their favorite restaurant. It is walking distance from their house, which sets the evening on a promising course. It turns out to be an otherwise nondescript Thai spot in a strip mall, but the promise is fulfilled with each staff member who greets them by name and each menu item that inspires a pause of appreciation on the first bite, then some restraint to keep our table from becoming a Thai food eating contest. When the husband and wife ownership team emerges from the kitchen to say hello, I wave off the Dedmons and tell the team I am their new biggest fan, which is not all that funny, but earns a big laugh anyway because everyone is enjoying themselves so much.

When the owners return to the kitchen, and it is down to the three of us once again, I raise a glass to the authenticity of the night, from the walk to the ingredients to the fellowship, and toast the alignment between our experience in this moment with how their son is determined to live his life.

"To the Philosophy of Phil," I announce.

They raise their glasses in kind.

The Dedmons are different people now. Not only compared to the frightened versions I drove to the hotel earlier, but to the people they had become over the course of our working relationship. Mrs. Dedmon's long sweater has been packed away, along with the worried look her husband wore as he stood ready at any moment to comfort her, his embrace adding another layer of protection to the one provided by the sweater. The confidence they carry since building a legacy in their son's name is now fortified with curiosity. Far from being afraid of the unknown, they enjoy getting to know it.

I drive southbound the next morning to visit June with the hope she will wind up with a comforting blend of her own. She may not have the confidence to pair with curiosity, but perhaps a mix of peace and faith is within her reach, or at least complacency and hope.

I rehearse a variety of ways to tell her about Elijah. Rather than the explicit unveiling granted to the Dedmons, which I hope they keep to themselves, this version of the afterlife will retain enough of its mystery to keep the debate alive should she feel compelled to share the story with anyone. And debate is essential for our system to function.

My phone starts to vibrate in the cup holder where I have it stashed for the drive. Enough messages arrive in sequence to make the phone scamper halfway around the circle by the time I stop in the parking lot of an outlet mall to stretch and check who sent them.

Rae is the messenger. The first text says she has been writing down her thoughts for days and is now ready to send them. She copied and pasted the passages into a series, rather than one long text, to help me process them.

"And to help myself process them too, honestly," she concedes. "I'm still wondering what I'm thinking about. That may not make sense, but not much seems to these days."

"I visited Britt and her grandma," the next text starts. "Thank you for offering to help, but I felt it was something I had to investigate on my own. I didn't want anyone around, no influences. My mind needed to be as open as possible in order to form a point of view on such an outlandish claim. I already have plenty of biases of my own when it comes to where we might go after we die, and how power operates when we're alive. Maybe I should have brought someone along who could call me on those filters, hold me to account. But I don't know who that person could be. It can't be you, and the circumstances are too ferocious for anyone else to access."

I click on the next bubble.

"You appealed to my biases when it comes to life after death, but the information comes from a place that repels me. The path of ambition my husband and I were on fell short of truly powerful circles before we were derailed, but I got close enough to feel a chill that makes me think I still would have used Rory's birth as an excuse to tap out, like I am now. I would have poured my energy into motherhood rather than into our foundation."

I start to wander along the storefronts as I tap on the next verse.

"Britt is adorable. She's curious, talkative, exceeding all the benchmarks for a girl her age. But the back seat of the Jeep and the dirty couches hover over all of it. Grandma shouldn't have been a grandma for another twenty years. She's still a cocktail waitress at a casino, but already looks older than my grandma. She keeps the wreckage running okay, but it's a lot of effort, and comes at the expense of Britt's childhood. It's too easy but also absolutely rational to fear that Britt will end up on the same wheel. The kid is exceptional, but up against a well-established rule. Her intelligence is a big part of what makes her so cute, but that brainpower will lead her to learn faster than most kids where she stands in the world, and instead of cute, she'll be sad and angry sooner than I care to think about."

I sit on a bench in front of a furniture warehouse where, according to the signs, everything must go.

"I spent several days in their world trying to find them," she begins the following text. "And several more getting to know them. I made up a backstory I thought would keep people from getting jumpy as I poked around. I knew I couldn't pretend to be one of them. They'd see right through me. So I said I worked for a foundation, that much was true, but one dedicated to studying universal basic income, and Brittania's grandma was one of the people chosen to see how much of a difference five hundred dollars per month would make in their lives. I played dumb about Britt. Never mentioned her. It worked. Rather than warn them about me, their buddies encouraged them to find me."

I tap the last text.

"When I met Britt, I did feel something. But it wasn't a cosmic connection, or whatever we choose to call that possibility. I didn't feel Rory's presence. All I felt was pity. I didn't see Rory's life in her eyes. I saw a kid with so much going for her, going nowhere. It was a helpless feeling. I don't know if there's any truth to what you told me, even a shred. So what if there is none? What if this is a scam? I've decided I don't care. If you think I need an elaborate story to compel me to do the right thing, so be it. The result is what matters. I may never believe she fits into some kind of universal grid, or on a karma scoreboard, but this girl is in my life now, and she needs help that I can provide. If she is the spirit of my child, she has made that spirit her own, and it deserves a chance to flourish."

There is a bit more to the text, but I stand up and take a walk.

It starts as a celebration, a victory lap, but becomes more reflective. Every step brings the two impulses together, a celebration of tranquility. I reach the edge of the last building and turn the corner to the other side. I wind up in back and find the end of the development. There is nothing more. Beyond the pavement is a windswept plain with blurry mountains on a distant horizon.

I hold up the last lines and read them. She thanks me for introducing her to Britt, and looks forward to finding a cure for the condition that took Rory.

I wonder how to reply to a collection of texts that comes to a conclusion about what matters in life. I am in no position to match her meditation, and offering a mere "right on!" or "see you at the next meeting!" would fall rightfully flat. I need to pack a lot of weight into a small space. After several waves of wind roll through the grasslands in front of me, I decide to tell her she has wisdom in abundance, and that I look forward to seeing where her work takes the world.

Trusting that her lack of a reply to my reply is a case of no news being good news, I resume my journey to June.

Dealing with the Dedmons and with Rae now seems easy compared to what awaits me over lunch next to the canyon. With no hard feelings and nothing unresolved between the Dedmons, and with Rae still able to idealize what could have been and what may be, in each case the children did the heavy lifting. All I did was set up the meetings. But June and Eli have none of the above. Their relationship was both lengthy and elusive, loaded with anxiety, and I need to stall until they meet again, whenever that ends up being.

I wait for June in our usual place, at our favorite table, armed with a painstaking clarity of how I am going to deliver the news that her son is dead.

She will not be surprised to hear Eli visited me in a dream, but bracing herself does not prevent the blow. Expectations can only cushion the landing so much. The pain will cave in on her. She will tell herself how stupid she was for thinking there was a chance, that she was living a lie by believing anything other than the inevitable.

So when she is ready for the details of my encounter with Eli, for most of the story I rely on my side of it. I tell her he talked to me during one of those restless nights when I wonder if I am on a good path in life, if the people I care about are safe, if I am spending my money wisely, if I have enough of it to carry out what I want to accomplish. I was bound for a night of worst-case scenarios. The kind of night that leads to being tired the next day, and later on relieved to rediscover that going about what needs to be done during the day can take away the concerns of the night.

But in this case, her son soothed me before the sun rose. He offered assurances that often relied on clichés, variations on climbing mountains and crossing deserts and parting clouds, but they worked because of who was saying them. I experienced every mountaintop and oasis in the desert and ray of sunshine in every word. If he had made up a metaphor of his own that was pure babble, I still would have found it soothing. He could make gibberish reassuring by his presence.

June emerges from the walking path on the other side of the parking lot. I wave and remind myself what I want to tell her at the end of the story.

Her son turned out to be the man he was meant to be after all, and I suspect she will see for herself someday. If she replies by saying she will let me know in my dreams, in so many words, in whatever tone, I have my answer. My work is done.

"Hello, Devin," she greets me as I stand to give her a hug.

Also by Sean Boling

The Current Mr. Orr
Devin's Best Afterlife
Once in Two Lifetimes
Revenge and Wellness in the Sweet Hereafter

Standalone
Cut Flowers
Abraham the Anchor Baby Terrorist
The Summer of Our Foreclosure
Satellite Campus
A Charter to That Other Place
The Latest Version of My Love Story
Show Them What They Won
The Name Field
Should
Moral Adjacent
Over Here We Have
The Current Mr. Orr

About the Author

Sean lives with his family in Templeton, California. He teaches English at Cuesta College.